EASEFUL DEATH

EASEFUL DEATH

RALPH MCINERNY

ATHENEUM
NEW YORK 1991
MAXWELL MACMILLAN CANADA
TORONTO
MAXWELL MACMILLAN INTERNATIONAL
NEW YORK OXFORD SINGAPORE SYDNEY

Atheneum
Macmillan Publishing Company
866 Third Avenue
New York, NY 10022

Maxwell Macmillan Canada, Inc.
1200 Eglinton Avenue East
Suite 200
Don Mills, Ontario M3C 3N1

Macmillan Publishing Company is part of the Maxwell Communication Group of Companies.

Library of Congress Cataloging-in-Publication Data

McInerny, Ralph M.
  Easeful death / Ralph McInerny.
    p.   cm.
  ISBN 0-689-12131-8
  I. Title.
PS3563.A31166E2   1991
813'.54—dc20   91-9962
                                                    CIP

10 9 8 7 6 5 4 3 2 1

Printed in the United States of America

For Karen and Mike Novak

For many a time
I have been half in love with easeful Death,
Called him soft names in many a mused rhyme,
To take into the air my quiet breath;
Now more than ever seems it rich to die,
To cease upon the midnight with no pain.

—*John Keats*

EASEFUL DEATH

Prologue

NOISES OUT behind the barn during the day, at night the flicker of a campfire in the woods north of the house, one rainy morning the indistinct trace of someone who'd been wandering around the yard during the night—Webster noted them all, husbanding the evidence like a wavering believer fashioning an argument for the existence of God. And then one cold but sunny day he saw the tramp rummaging around in the trash at the end of the drive and went down to talk to him.

"Can I help you?"

The head did not lift but eyes appeared above the thick glasses, a wild animal looking through Blakeian underbrush. He had already extracted several bottles with amounts of liquor so minuscule they would have to be measured in microgills. Webster felt a reluctant solidarity with the bedraggled stranger.

"You want a drink, come up to the house."

Walking away, not looking back, he wondered if the man would follow. It was like taking a chance in the cosmic

lottery, or more likely advancing through a determined uni-
verse where adventure consists in our ignorance of the neces-
sity with which we act. If we're in control of our lives, how
the hell had he ended up rusticating on a farm north of
Madison, Wisconsin?

At the house he turned. The tramp had taken several steps
up the drive but stopped when Webster looked back. The
poet waved him on. It is not good for man to drink alone.

That is how it began.

His name was Ober, or so he said in payment for the can
of beer Webster tossed to him when he came onto the porch.
How long since the hand holding the can had been washed?
Or the body to which the arm to which the hand belonged,
for that matter? Ober's clothing fit him like an animal pelt
rather than garments that were doffed and donned with regu-
larity. His shoes had a chthonic look, as much mud and grit
as leather showing.

"Where you going?"

A ticlike movement squinted one eye and a shoulder lifted.
"The name was originally Oberman. My father changed it."

"Superman."

Teeth ranging from light yellow to dark brown appeared
and disappeared. *"Ja."*

"That you camping in the north woods?"

"North of what?"

"You want to do some chores, chopping wood, cleaning
up . . ."

But Ober shook his head. "I'm retired."

"From what?"

"The human race."

"So am I."

Ober looked around, his hand crushing the can as he did.
"You got a better retirement plan than I do."

He supposed it looked better—it *was* better; it was romantic to imagine that he and Ober were in the same circum-

stances—but was he really better off? A roof over his head, no wolf at the door, three squares a day aside, how did they differ essentially? Ober was going nowhere and neither was he. Maybe the difference was he had been somewhere once.

After his long-ago discharge from the navy Ober had stayed on in a California that made his native Iowa seem pale, flat and unprofitable.

"Shakespeare?"

"No, Long Beach." Again the yellow and brown teeth.

"Doing what?"

"As little as possible."

Ober's epiphany had come at a platoon beer party held on the beach at San Juan Capistrano when with a pleasant buzz on he had watched a couple emerge from a car drawn onto the shoulder of 101 and walk hand in hand down to the water.

"In bathing suits. They were in their forties, I suppose, but they seemed a magic combination of old and young to me, a symbol of the state. Living there made you immortal, that's more or less what I thought."

"So you become immortal."

"Well, I always had a good tan."

He had also had one earthquake too many. "What's the point of not growing old if the earth can open up and swallow you any time it wants?"

"It will anyway."

"That's right."

"How old are you?"

"Your age."

Webster felt resentment. The suggestion that he was as old as this old man of the road was offensive, but only mildly so. He found he liked the sense of solidarity he felt with Ober. Solidarity *cum* superiority, of course, *über oberman*.

"I'm in my seventh decade," Ober said.

"Seventy what?"

"Not my eighth, my seventh decade."

In his sixties! "What a hell of a way to put it."

"So I'm right about our ages."

"If you're telling the truth. I'm sixty-one."

"Then we're exactly the same."

Webster didn't believe him. If he had said he was sixty-five, he was sure the tramp would have claimed to be that age. Ober put the empty crushed can into the pocket of his overcoat. Being neat? It turned out he wanted the recycling redemption. What was it like to have a few cents matter?

They had three beers before Ober shuffled down the drive. Webster watched him go almost with regret. Vague thoughts of using Ober came and went. It was a cliché. The drunk in the furnace. Quizzing the streetwalker on how she had gotten into the life. Ober had lazed his life away on the beaches of California and now had wandered back to the Midwest, probably one more search for his lost youth. Maybe if Webster had been writing at the time he would have done something with his odd visitor.

> A mild mendicant begs the question
> Of his raison d'être, speaking fustian
> On my porch . . .

It petered out as ideas had of late. Of late! In recent years. But the experience was to find its voice in prose, an imaginary journal, a new departure for Webster.

After that first visit Webster looked in vain for firelight in the north woods, but there was only the damp chilly night at his window. He did not want to think of Ober, or anyone else, out in weather like that.

The following night, he left the doors of the barn open and the next day at noon Ober came yawning out of them into the feeble sunlight. He took the sandwiches Webster offered, put them into his pocket, and shouldered the backpack that was oddly reminiscent of those of the students Webster had fled.

"Eat those here. I'll give you more for the road."

" 'I will build me a house by the side of the road and be a friend to man.' "

Webster winced. "Where did you sleep the night before last?"

Ober answered with a question of his own. "What are you retired from?"

How to put it? Webster had never considered teaching his career; the series of university appointments had been sinecures enabling him to write. And to teach writing to the young. Which is as impossible as teaching writing to the old. Webster had been willing to exploit the crazy notion that writing poetry and fiction was just another trade that schools could teach, but of course he hadn't believed it. From time to time students with genuine talent wandered into his class, but he quickly converted them into friends, got them out of the classroom, encouraged them to write untrammeled by the pap he dished out to those whose only gain from the course would be three dubious credits.

Kids like Eric who left in junior year, rode a barge down the Mississippi to New Orleans and shipped out to Argentina, eventually transmuting it all into a manuscript that was neither fiction nor nonfiction, or maybe it was both. Eric was hailed as the new Twain, the new Thoreau, the new Theroux. Alas, *Anabasis* was all he wrote. He went on to India and died, all drugged out before he was thirty.

The girls were different. By and large they had used their talent, their literary talent, and gone on to something like a career. Sharon Whatzhername went into publishing but vatic poems of hers continued to appear infrequently in *The New Yorker*. Hazel, whose reviews were works of art and much sought after, and very very long. And Inez, who maybe could still become a poet but had been betrayed so far by her subject matter. Her life simply wasn't interesting enough to generate first-rate stuff. After their semester of fortnightly rolls in the hay, Inez had settled into the dullness of a business career. She should have married and gone to Skokie and had kids, something real. Or chosen a city other than Chicago.

"I retired from being poet-in-residence."

Ober waited and Webster wasn't sure he wanted to confide in the tramp. Once he started where would he stop? The answer to that turned out to be that he wouldn't stop. Those sessions on the back porch were therapy, confession, an oral autobiography, the search for sense in his life. "To Carthage then I came. Meaning Madison."

"You had not thought death had undone so many."

Retorts like that pricked his interest in Ober. "Did you go to school after the navy?" By then he knew that Ober while a seaman had taken correspondence courses from the Naval Institute in literature and history.

"Some weekends I wintered in the mountains above San Bernardino where I was tutored by coeds."

So they had that in common as well, two old ass hounds sitting on a Wisconsin porch, talking their lives into shape.

Their sessions escalated from beer to Scotch, a mistake, being on beer was like being on the wagon. The bottles Ober had dug from the trash that first visit were long dead soldiers, just a matter of getting rid of stuff cluttering up the cupboards. Talking with Ober was as good or better than the old times they reminded Webster of. But talking with students was always half a con job. The credulous young can be told anything and he told them anything, anything but the whole truth.

After a week, Ober asked to wash up and Webster gave him some of his own clothes. A great improvement. Talking to a man wearing his own clothes was odd, but then he had come to think of these sessions as a species of talking to himself. Did Ober really listen? Why should the man care?

He was warm and fed and full of booze for the first time in who knew how long, so why shouldn't he nod through Webster's monologues?

Ober moved into the room off the kitchen, once a maid's room. Webster couldn't ask the man to go out to the barn after a night spent shooting the bull. Particularly when he nodded off in his chair.

> My altered ego falls asleep
> Lulled by tales that make the teller weep . . .

Words that came easily were doggerel and better ones would not be summoned no matter how late he sat up half drunk at his desk. He began to speak to Ober when he wasn't there. Is that what the tramp had saved him from, the eccentricity of one living alone, talking endlessly to himself?

Ober took a volume of Webster's poetry from the shelf and spent most of an afternoon with it.

"What do you think?"

Ober shrugged. "You try too hard."

Anger boiled up in him. Who the hell did Ober think he was, dismissing a whole volume of poems representing years of work with a goddam stupid remark like that?

"When you don't, I like them."

"Give me an example." How swiftly his disposition altered at the prospect of praise. It did not seem absurd to want Ober's praise, however offensive his criticism had seemed. Ober cited "Villanelle" as one he liked. Had he any idea how technically complicated the poem was? All the more reason to rejoice that he had created the illusion of ease, as if he had dashed it off.

"Read it," Webster suggested, but Ober handed the book to him.

"It's your poem."

Webster knew his reading voice was good. How much of

such reputation as he had was due to the way he read his poems? His own and others. He had developed a little program of verse and taken it on tour. And then recorded some on cassettes, something to be hustled along with copies of the books after the reading. Those readings relieved the oppressive realization of how many technically good poets were currently writing. The average level of poetry was, he sometimes thought, higher than it had ever been before, but greatness was missing, missing from his own stuff, too, he knew it, he tried to reconcile himself to the fact that he was a minor poet in a crowded field. Cyril Connolly once defined success as writing a book that would still be read ten years after its appearance. Webster knew how difficult that apparently modest goal was to achieve. But public readings created the illusion that he was the only bard in the world.

"And I am the only girl."

Deborah, wasn't it? The toothy blonde from Keokuk who hung on and on after he was through reading and got asked along to the dinner in the Italian restaurant and offered to drive him to the motel. He had been explaining to her how he felt on the road reading and she had sung those words to the tune of the appropriate song, flinging off the sheet as she sang. Ah, the one night stands. But why had he remembered Deborah? If that was her name. It was the flamboyant gesture he remembered.

"When did you write that?" Ober asked after he finished reading "Villanelle."

"A long time ago."

"Where is your recent stuff?"

There had been one collection after the book that contained "Villanelle," but that was fifteen years ago.

"I haven't collected it yet."

"Is that what you do all day, write poetry?"

But what he had started to do was write a prose work, a thinly disguised fictional account of Ober's arrival and his own growing sense that the man was somehow the mirror of his soul, some self he might have been. And vice versa. It was a Conradian theme, he recognized that, and expelled the recognition. It was the bane of the literary life, art imitated art rather than nature. But he sat at his desk as if he were Marlow telling his drinking companions of Ober's arrival. This served to confer new importance on his houseguest, as if he were a character in search of a plot. The plot that formed on the pages as he wrote was one in which the narrator felt more and more oppressed by the presence of this alternate self, felt his memories becoming part of a possible world he himself did not inhabit. The narrator's sense grew that unless he got rid of his guest a day would come when there would no longer be two of them, just one, and that one would be the visitor. Not Conrad, Hawthorne. But he no longer cared about antecedents or similarities. The story became his own. The narrator became convinced that he must evict his guest. But no, that was no solution. It was Ober or himself. Ober must die.

When they sat together drinking, Webster wondered what Ober would think of the strange story he was making out of their life together. Life together. He had tried to live with others before and, like a wife, Ober began to grate on his nerves. It was nothing that could become an indictment, only the quotidian quota of annoying otherness, a personality not his own in the house, asserting itself, just being there. His wives had wanted to know what specifically had gone wrong when things fell apart, but it was never anything specific, it was the general idea of being linked to another person.

> Stoned in a glass house, I mirror
> As I am mirrored, am queer or
> Quaint, image of an image,
> Neither real nor of the other judge.

But it was his prose account that mattered now, his sense that his soul was slipping through his pores, inhabiting Ober, much as he in listening to the other man felt that this vicarious experience was all he had now. The drinking did not help. Webster was a bad drunk but Ober was worse, a raging, destructive animal, bellicose, stewing for a fight. More in anger than fear, Webster locked the door when Ober reeled onto the back porch and began to piss in a high arc over the railing and onto the lawn, bellowing as he did so. When he turned to come in again, the locked door puzzled him at first, then enraged him. He beat on the door for minutes before bringing his closed fists against the window and smashing it. Webster, armed with a deer rifle, faced Ober.

"Get the hell out of here, you sonofabitch. Now. Out."

And he lifted the rifle and fired over Ober's head, the roar sobering them both. Ober slumped to the porch and began to weep, a mewling, pathetic, self-pitying sound that made Webster want to lower the rifle and blast that bawling beast off his porch. But he pulled the rifle in through the broken window, turned off the porch and kitchen lights and went into the library where without warning all his drunkenness returned. He sat on the couch. The room revolved wildly. He felt ill. He inhaled deeply and held his breath. A moment later he swooned sideways onto the couch and slept.

He was up at five, his mind clear and full of the final scenes in the fictional version of what was happening. It was only a matter of getting them down; they had written themselves in his head during his drunken sleep.

In the morning he awoke and came unsteadily downstairs to find the house deserted. He moved from room to room, scarcely able to believe his luck. The kitchen door stood open, left ajar by his departing nemesis. He went onto the porch and looked down the drive to the road. Relief gave way to sadness. Standing in the rumpled clothes he'd slept in, he lifted an arm to wave farewell and it was like seeing off his own soul, like being on shore while Charon poled his boat out across the stygian waters and the moans of the damned drifted back to him.

Finis. The end. He had finished *The Leaden Echo*. There would be no sequel, no golden echo. This was the longest piece of prose fiction he had ever written and he had no desire to repeat the performance.

Ending the notebook exorcised the house of Ober's presence. In the kitchen shards of glass lay on the linoleum floor. Webster stood first at one window and then another, looking out. There was no sign of Ober. He unlocked the door and went across the porch and stood like the narrator of his journal looking down to the road. Had Ober weaved his way down that drive in the dark and continued on into the night? He felt no twinge of sadness. But when he turned, he looked out at the barn. Its doors were closed. It had been days since Ober had slept in the barn. The thought grew on him that Ober was out there. He still wasn't rid of him.

He went across the yard, shielding his eyes from the sun that stood at ten o'clock in the cloudless sky. The barn doors were tightly closed. Would Ober have bothered to shut them at all, let alone so tightly? He levered down the latch with his thumb and tugged the great door open. A bird flew out with an excited flutter and Webster stepped back. He might have been seeking a better perspective. The now-open doors provided a frame, but because of the sun it was impossible to see inside. Webster stepped into the shadow of the barn.

The body hung from a beam that formed the outer edge of the loft. Because of the clothes Ober wore Webster's first crazy thought was that it was he himself who hung lifeless there, black tongue protruding from his slack mouth, his body nothing but weight now, the shoes tipped downward. He pulled the doors shut behind him and was alone with the dead body of his alter ego.

BOOK ONE

PART ONE

FROM THE library, two doors, one on either side of the fireplace, led to a sun porch Webster had converted into his study. There the poet had sat at a trestle table, his back to the one unwindowed wall of the porch, able to be distracted in three directions by the views to north and west and south. And here Clinton, the curator of the papers, ensconced himself in the precise place where Webster had created his best work. What an almost religious sensation it had been to read the "Baraboo Elegies" seated at the very table on which they had been composed, in the exact time of year that the first had been written. This ceremonial reading had taken place the previous October when a sense of oneness with the late poet, of being somehow Webster's continuation in time, first took possession of Clinton. That sense had been strengthened since as he immersed himself in the flotsam and jetsam of a literary life, boxes and boxes filled with every scrap and note, every draft, every success and every failure. Clinton came almost to resent the work that Aran, Webster's third and, as he always added, final wife, had done during her brief tenure. Of course she had scarcely begun to put what she conceived to be order into the papers before the poet's uxorial attention span had begun to weaken, she was deprived of the thought that she and she alone occupied his amorous regard and, inevitably, as everyone had predicted, the marriage came to an acrimonious conclusion whose aftermath was played out in a Madison courtroom. Aran sought the lion's share of a nonexistent fortune while Webster countered with the charge that she had introduced chaos into his manuscripts. Aran got no fortune and Webster restored disorder to his papers. Webster in his charge had referred to his recent work. If any such poems existed they would have been the only completed work in the prolonged period of drought that had preceded the poet's suicide nearly two years ago. Webster's handwritten valedictory to the world hung framed on the wall behind the chair in which Clinton worked.

> Choosing not to let my death unchosen
> Come, I summon it as servant to my will;
> Say this, and then forever to the still
> Stygian depths my body frozen
> Give
> That dying thus I'll live . . .

Had he as he signed this realized it was the last time he would trace with ink upon a page his famous name? The ashes in the charred ruin of the pyre on which he had immolated himself were sufficient to justify the issuance of the death certificate. A repentant Aran recalled the poet saying that the only convincing argument against suicide was that it left a mess for others to clean up. He had chosen a method to spare others. In the neighborhood there were those who claimed to have seen the flaming pyre in the distance. By the time the village fire truck arrived the flames had passed their peak. The volunteer crew stood watching the fire die

down, gutter, go out, little suspecting that they were atten-
dants at the first obsequies the last remains of Webster would
receive. Memorial services had been held in half a dozen
locations around the country at which selections from
Webster's oeuvre were read to pensive gatherings. On the
mantel in the library was a simple vase, once brought by
Webster from Mexico, containing ashes which were taken to
be those of the poet.

Webster's way of leaving the world had done wonders for
his posthumous reputation. The news stories drew the attention of many to his poetry who otherwise might never have
heard of him. One of the newsmagazines devoted a cover
story to the man and his work, old rivals came forward to
confess their affection for the poet and admiration for his
work, anecdotes were dusted off and told to newly interested
listeners. The University of Wisconsin prepared a traveling
exhibit that still traversed the country, bringing to thousands
the poetry of Webster as well as the antic tale of his life.
The irresponsibility of his womanizing, his legendary alco-
holism, his pettiness—all were swallowed up in the dramatic
ending of the poet's life which cast retroactive light on everything that went before it. Howard Webster became in death
a mythical figure.

The Webster Foundation benefited from the fortune that
Aran had wrongly believed to exist before but came to exist
then. Cassettes in which, largely for his own edification,
Webster had read his works were issued in an album, in
cassettes and on CD's, and knew a phenomenal sale. But
the real bonanza proved to be the prose work Webster had
left in manuscript. Issued with an introduction by Saul
Bellow, the book to everyone's surprise instantly became a
best-seller, stayed among the top ten for eight months and,
in paperback, enjoyed another life. Within a year of publication, there were a million copies of *The Leaden Echo* in
print. Felicia, Webster's daughter by his first wife, oversaw

the establishment of the Webster Foundation. The house, she decided, would become the archives of her father's papers, a curator and custodian would be required. Albert Clinton applied for and beat out three other applicants for the job. A year ago he and Jane had moved in.

She had been as excited by the idea as he was when the letter from the Webster Foundation arrived asking if he would like to be a candidate for the position. He was then on a nontenure track on one of the lesser campuses of the University of Wisconsin system, where the fact that he had written his dissertation on Webster's "Elegies" was of no interest to the earnest 4-H Club types he taught. His name had been proposed to the Webster Foundation by Professor Gregory, director of his dissertation. Clinton answered in the affirmative and tried to develop a stoic ataraxy as he waited. If he hoped for nothing he could not be disappointed. Jane, who had not been to church in years, lit vigil lights once a day in St. Bartholomew's Church and began a novena to Saint Anthony of Padua.

"Saint Anthony?"

"The nuns told us he never fails."

"At what?"

"Getting you what you want."

"Do you really believe that?"

"Wait and see."

He waited and saw. He was asked to come for an interview at which he thought he did badly, but a week later he was offered the job over the phone and was given twenty-four hours to make up his mind.

"It's made up. I accept."

Jane insisted that he go with her to St. Bartholomew's to light a candle of thanksgiving. He would have relit Webster's funeral pyre, he was so giddy with gratitude. He turned in his resignation immediately, smiled through the department chair's protest. He was burning his bridges as well as vigil lights. His career had taken an unexpected and upward turn and he had no intention of apologizing to the Trout Lake Campus for any inconvenience his departure caused.

Their first weeks in the house had been the honeymoon they couldn't afford when they married. Jane wandered through the rooms, unable to believe their luck.

"These floors are oak," she marveled.

She loved everything about it, even the old-fashioned kitchen with its walk-in pantry and wood stove, its high windows that looked west so that after supper they sat on at the table to watch a golden sun drop through the trees and end another perfect day. She had been as excited as he was when he came upon the prose work that was the last thing Howard Webster had written. When the first snow fell Jane was ecstatic. Clinton woke to find her standing at the window, hugging her flanneled self with delight as she gazed out at the snowflakes dreamily drifting down. After breakfast, when he went to the study, she wandered out across the yard, wading through the drifts, down through a pasture, toward the woods. The spell was broken when a dog came snarling out of the underbrush and scared the hell out of her. Her screams reached him in the study and he ran outside dressed as he was, house slippers, an old cardigan, corduroys. Snow crept up his pant legs, filled his slippers, twice he fell, but he continued on to his terrified wife, shouting as he came. The dog waited with cocked head. Clinton, filled with enraged valor, ran at the beast, bellowing like a bull. The dog, a setter of sorts, backed away, turned and disappeared. Jane came sobbing into his arms and they made their way back to the house, leaning against one another. The cold he caught lasted a week. Jane refused to talk about her encounter with the dog. Life at the house was never the same again.

The relationship between spouses became a relationship between adversaries. From time to time arguments broke

out—Jane now professed to have had misgivings from the
beginning about moving to this godforsaken part of the state,
far from a sizable town let alone city, without friends or
diversion—but these outbursts were almost a relief from the
long silent days when they would meet only to dine word-
lessly, then avoid one another's company. Jane would slip
away to bed before him and be asleep or feigning sleep when
he came up the wide creaking stairs to their bedroom.

"Would you like to live in Waverly?" he asked, seeking
compromise. He did not want to move to the village but
how could they go on like this?

"Waverly!" Her mouth opened in disbelief.

"It wouldn't be so lonesome. There'd be things to do,
other people . . ."

She turned and left him, his suggestion beneath contempt,
but later that day she came into the study, sat and waited
for him to finish what he was doing.

"We could live in Madison," she said.

He straightened his notes, moved the shoe box from which
he had taken them. "Madison is seventy-five miles away."

"People drive that distance all the time, New Yorkers,
Californians . . ."

"That would be a hundred and fifty miles a day."

"You wouldn't have to come up every day."

"Jane, this is my job!"

She rose to her feet, all icy calmness. "That's right! It's
your job. But what in the name of God am I supposed to
do here? I can't even go outside without being attacked by
wild dogs."

Idiotically, he bought her a dog, as if that might somehow
solve things. They had talked of having children after they
moved in and were settled in their new life. The little spaniel
urinated on everything and whimpered in the night and three
days after bringing it home Clinton returned it to the kennel.

"Sumpin wrong?"

"We're worried about neighbor dogs."

"Hell, dogs like dogs."

"You don't know the one I mean."

The man made an effort to find out, angry to lose the sale, and some days later a pickup pulled into the drive with the dog that had frightened Jane seated beside the driver. This was Harris, their neighbor. He got out of the truck and his dog bounded out with him. Clinton was watching this from the study window but the dog brought a scream from the kitchen. He collided with Jane as he ran to the back door and held her trembling against him. It was as intimate as they had been in weeks, terror now overcoming her determination to deprive him of affection.

"A man is here with that dog."

"I'll see about it."

The dog frolicked about like a puppy while Clinton talked with Harris, a man of thirty whose face was weatherworn and whose morning shave had left tufts of black hair sprouting from his jawline. Clinton told Harris his dog had frightened his wife when she was walking in the woods.

"Bessie? She wouldn't hurt a flea."

"You know women," Clinton said disloyally.

"Well, I know dogs. Not the same thing." His smile revealed a gap in his lower teeth. "You ought to get the missus a dog, a real dog, not a spaniel." So Gill had told him.

"Maybe we will."

"What sort of work you do?"

"Did you know Webster when he lived here?"

"I can't say I knew him. He kept pretty much to himself. Hit the bottle pretty good."

"He was a famous poet."

"You know how he went? Climbed up on top of a stack of wood and lit the goddam thing. Brightened the countryside for miles around." Harris smiled. "What's he got to do with you?"

"I'm in charge of his papers."

Harris obviously wondered if his leg was being pulled. But then he thought he had it. "You a lawyer?"

"I'm looking after the estate."

"Estate?" Harris pushed back his cap and looked around.

No point in trying to explain the foundation and archives and the rest of it to Harris. If Clinton had needed any reminder of the gulf that opened between him and his neighbors, Harris would have been sufficient reminder. How the hell had Webster managed to live here for a dozen years? The rustic stood there, waiting for an intelligible explanation. Clinton's cup of coffee had cooled and he dumped the contents on the ground. Harris followed this. Their eyes met. Did he expect to be offered a cup of coffee? Clinton could not read the man. But when he went inside he said nothing, not wanting to fuel Jane's already inflamed discontent.

Later that night he told her they would drive down to Madison and look into the possibility of living there.

"You're not resigning?" Hope and horror mixed in her voice: too complete a victory would be a species of defeat.

"No, I'll commute."

2

FELICIA'S MOOD was as cheerful as the metallic gray surface of Lake Michigan that lay below the nineteenth-floor conference room of Haver, Rowes and Cannon. Cannon had been a boyhood friend of her father's in Ellsworth, her reason for turning to him when royalties began pouring in and the idea of the foundation formed in her mind. The last thing she wanted was more money with which to spoil her children. Frank already earned more than enough for that but he did not like the idea of the foundation.

"Why Haver, Rowes and Cannon?"

"Cannon and my father were boys together."

"Well, I guess that's a reason." Meaning not a good one, but this was something she had not wanted to depend on Frank for. Her father's sudden posthumous reputation and wealth had given her a renewed sense of being someone in her own right. Frank's lack of enthusiasm for the law firm of Haver, Rowes and Cannon had given her pause, but she had overridden her doubts. This decision would be hers alone. And so it had been, and now seated in the conference room listening to Cannon read the financial report she had the sense that it had all somehow been wrested from her. The foundation was effectively controlled by Cannon and his flunky Baum. They each had a vote and she had only one. She had prevailed on the hiring of Albert Clinton but since then she felt more a spectator than a participant in the Webster Foundation.

"I want there to be Webster fellowships."

Cannon sat with his back to the window, leaving his face in shadow and difficult to interpret. He said nothing, nor did Baum. Did they think the remark would just be stricken from the record if she said nothing more?

"Grants to young poets."

"I don't like it," Cannon said, "and I'll tell you why. You think your dad depended on handouts to make his career? Uh uh. Fact is, I think he would have refused any kind of help he hadn't earned."

"He had two NEA grants," Felicia said.

"After he was established. I'm talking about Howard young. You said young poets."

The most annoying thing about Cannon was his intimation that he had known her father well and could interpret his wishes infallibly. They may have been boys together in Ellsworth but so far as Felicia knew their paths had diverged at the university and they had never seen one another again.

"He always helped young poets."

Felicia said it with finality, not because she thought it was true—save in the case of aspiring young female poets—but because she did not intend to let Cannon deflect her from her purpose. In the year and a half since her father's death, her own memories of him were being replaced by the benevolent, almost mythical figure suggested by the Webster Foundation. The solidity of the legal institution contradicted her father's lifelong indifference to obligations and laws, both civil and moral. His consuming egoism had permitted him to sacrifice everyone and everything to his supposed talent. It had never been a settled thing in his lifetime that he was anything more than a second-rate poet; indeed, there were critics who would not grant him even that. That she and her mother had suffered, that creditors had gone unpaid, all for nought, was worse than irony, but now after his death Howard Webster unexpectedly had been admitted to the pantheon, he was written of in tones of awe, he was both a critical and a commercial success. Felicia did not really wish her mother had lived to see this complete reversal of a philandering husband's reputation—poor Vivian would have preferred a public recognition of what a scoundrel he had been—but for herself Felicia far preferred this modified version of her father. Fellowships for young poets very definitely fit the image of him that the foundation was meant to promote.

"You heard the financial report, Felicia."

"I'm thinking of an open competition, selections to be made by a committee, quite a bit of hoopla."

"We can't afford it."

"Can't afford it! Be serious. I know how much money I put into the foundation."

"Of which we are legally required to spend the income and a percentage of the corpus. We are fully committed for the year."

"I did not imagine grants would be made immediately."

"This year's commitments will be duplicated next year."

"But we're not doing anything yet."

Cannon left it to Baum to spell it out for her. The upkeep and repairs to the house, the salary to young Clinton, coupled with a very shaky market, made it look probable that next year would with luck be equal to the present.

"Then we will dip into the corpus."

She might have sworn in church. Cannon shook his head.

"Felicia, no one in the world would advise us to do a thing like that."

After ten minutes more of such intransigence, Felicia got to her feet and shoved papers into the briefcase she had bought as an emblem of her new autonomy. Her impulse was to demand a formal vote but the outcome would be two to one against and then where would she be? How foolish she had been to agree to Baum as secretary-treasurer, the third officer of the foundation.

"I'll see what advice I get."

Cannon scrambled to his feet and came with her as she strode out of the conference room and headed for the reception area. His excitement was the only compensation she had for being prevented from doing what she wanted to do. Cannon was supposed to be her lawyer, but for all practical purposes she had been turned into his ineffectual appendage.

"Advice from whom, Felicia? You mustn't be telling all and sundry the business of the foundation."

She smiled sweetly at him. "A lawyer will be bound by professional secrecy."

"A lawyer! But I'm your lawyer."

"You have put your finger on my problem."

She felt good all the way down in the elevator. But in her car she sat wondering how she could carry out her threat. She might have talked it over with Frank, but that would be a double admission of defeat.

3

Mrs. Metzger came into his office, shut the door, and silently formed the word. *Hec-tor.* She had never said in so many words what she thought about his venture with Hector but her manner told Frank Leamon what she thought. It was what he thought himself, if he could be honest about it. It didn't matter. With sixty thousand sunk into Ultima Thule, in addition to at least a hundred and fifty in the three previous surefire ideas, he needed the cushion of Hector's involvement in this one.

"Give me a minute?"

"I could schedule him for tomorrow."

"No. No, I'll see him now."

He avoided her eyes. Alone, he told himself to cut his losses now. Throwing good money after bad had proved stupid again and again. All he had to do was swallow his pride and the loss of money Felicia had no idea he'd invested in schemes that made gold-mining stock in Queensland, Australia, look gilt-edged.

Why the hell was he such a sucker for get-rich-quick ideas? By any estimate he was a successful man. He couldn't be so deeply in debt if he weren't successful, and he didn't mean the money he owed Hector. The overhead for his office and warehouse, his payroll, Mrs. Metzger and the three people working for her, the mortgaged house, the boat, the cabin up north, the kids' tuition—once a quarter he confronted the high cost of success and had to fight dreams of sailing his boat right out the St. Lawrence seaway and following one of the round-the-world routes he'd mooned over while reading *Yachting*. The alternative to that was a quick hit with one of his enterprises. Geez. When he signaled Mrs. Metzger to send his visitor in, he didn't know whether he was going to tell Hector this was the end, he had no more venture capital, he was bailing out, or sing once more for his increasingly reluctant partner the siren song of eventual success.

Hector entered the room like the setting sun, half-hopeful smile, overweight, rumpled, a forty-six-year-old kid.

"I just signed up Andre Jouet!" Frank announced.

"Tell me about it." Hector fell into one of the leather chairs as if he had been dropped from the ceiling.

"We can have the whole line at forty percent off and advertise it as Jouet. With Baxter, Mr. George and Max Faber, this cinches it, Hector. Andre goes on the front cover, I've already told the printer to hold for new artwork."

"I thought they'd already printed the covers!"

Glossy, full-color, Frank himself had squirmed at the winning bid but convinced himself and Hector that they had to look as good as Land's End.

Hector levered himself upright as Frank dealt him photographs of the Andre Jouet line of men's clothing that they would be offering at forty percent off through their mail-order clothing business. Hector had turned his basement and garage into warehouses for the stock that had started to arrive, some on consignment, some bought outright for reduced prices. Direct mail was to be their route to riches, a first mailing of one hundred thousand catalogues cost a mere eighteen thousand dollars. A two percent return of two thousand orders at an average of one hundred dollars . . . Such appeals to avarice had undone Frank again and again. What had happened to the Classics on Cassettes scheme, Mrs. Metzger reading summaries of Dickens and Shakespeare and Twain that Frank had pirated from library reference books? He had found statistics on the amount of cassette tapes purchased each year, it was a growing market, the tapes a regular item in the bookstores in suburban malls. The initial investment had been small, at least until he talked himself into an ad campaign in the *New York Review of Books* that eventually ran to fifteen thousand dollars. The project had foundered on the problem of distribution. Frank's flowchart had been predicated on nonexistent water. Half a dozen independent book salesreps had taken on the line but when the orders came in they were for two or three copies of a single title. Frank had dreamt of dozens of copies of every title in every order. Even as the dream faded he became buoyant with a new scheme, one that would enable him to recoup his losses from Classics on Cassettes.

"I'm taking nothing out until I get my investment back," he assured Mrs. Metzger. "I don't care if it takes months."

Months! It had been two years and instead of getting his money back Frank had fed his fantasy of instant financial success again and again. Now Ultima Thule was going to bring money pouring in and remove all memories of past failure. Perhaps sharing the gamble with Hector would change his luck. Frank was an artist when it came to flowcharts, the march of income and expenditures displayed across successive months, the point at which investment turned to ever-increasing profits clearly marked. The mathematics of these charts was impeccable. But they had been the orchestration of factors that had failed to materialize, sales that were not made, income that did not come, percentages that had no real quantities to work on. If the future was like the past, Frank stood to lose another sixty thousand dollars. Or more. The reprinting of the catalogue cover meant another expense. If he had a rational bone in his body he would go with what they had, save Andre Jouet for the next catalogue, after the scheme had proved itself. He smiled when Hector predictably suggested this.

"I was tempted by the same thought, Hector. Believe me, the printer tried to convince me of much the same thing. He had already scheduled binding time and didn't want to screw up his schedule. This is one of those crucial moments, Hector. Sure we could go ahead with a pretty good catalogue and hope for the best. We could do that. But why run a race with one leg tied? We've come this far, Hector. I want Ultima Thule to be first-class from the start. Without Jouet we are second-class."

Frank spoke with patience, the old expert spelling it out for the neophyte. Hector should have known better. He taught night courses in business planning and spent his days managing the money he had been left by his surgeon father. He lived his life within the safe parameters of conservative investment but he was a poet of entrepreneurial capitalism, spoke with real emotion of cottage industries that had grown into multinational concerns. Did Frank know how McDonald's had begun? Of course Frank did. For Hector the world of business was a fantastic arena in which the downtrodden of this world rose inexorably to the top on the basis of grit, ideas and persistence. His own comfortable life contradicted this belief, but his faith was stronger for being based on fantasy. He was an ideal investment partner for Frank but under the pressure of experience his enthusiasm was waning. Whenever he had vowed to cut his ties to the sinking ship of Frank's latest scheme, he had been won back by the argument that this time Frank would make it big, everything would turn out in the way his flowcharts predicted, money would pour in upon them and all the reversals of the past be drowned in success. Ten minutes after he arrived, Hector was writing a check to appease the printer.

"If you had your late father-in-law's signature it might be worth as much as this check."

"Any banker would prefer your signature."

Hector's eyes rose dreamily to the ceiling. "I read the other day what a handwritten manuscript of one of Auden's poems brought at auction."

"How much?"

"Thousands."

He walked Hector out through Mrs. Metzger's office lest the secretary's baleful look turn the reluctant entrepreneur repentant. There was always the note of gratitude in Hector when he left the office. Frank's manner was that of the philanthropist who had let Hector in on a good thing. Frank prayed that this time he was right. He beat it back to his office, not looking Mrs. Metzger in the eye when he spoke to her.

"Get Holmer on the line, would you, please?"

Holmer owed him money and the call was meant to suggest that he was more creditor than debtor.

"Mr. Holmer is out of town," Mrs. Metzger told him a moment later.

"When do they expect him back?"

"I left a message."

He thanked her. No point in taking out his sense of being a con man on her. Holmer would have been different, the deadbeat deserved to be scapegoat for the anger Frank could not feel at Hector. Alone, he studied the screen of his computer for a time, but his thoughts were elsewhere, back at the recurrent problem. Why was he such a sucker for get-rich-quick schemes?

One of the Classics on Cassettes was Dostoevsky's *The Gambler* and Frank had recognized too much of himself in the hero's compulsive, doomed return to the gaming tables. Did he even expect one of his projects to succeed? The excursions out of character, playing entrepreneur to Hector although he was in the practice of law as hardheaded as they come, seemed a mad effort to negate the success he had known. But then the posthumous career of Felicia's father had seemed to mock all his energetic efforts.

1 PART TWO

TREES FLANKED the main street and met overhead, creating a bowered tunnel through which at midday only the smallest slivers of sun penetrated to the indolent Sardinians in repose on benches, in doorways, at café tables, leaning against parked cars. This island was a smaller island off the southwest coast of Sardinia to which he had driven from Cagliari, wearied of the seaport with its mad traffic, noise and smells. Besides, the town was hilly, walking too exhausting for a dead man. So he rented a car and drove a winding westward road to Sant'Antioco.

He had driven through the town to the far side of the island, looking for some resort hotel awaiting the season, but the coast was not at all like that he had come along from Cagliari and he returned to the town and its tunnel of trees and noontime twilight.

His room was on that shaded street, in a hotel whose lobby was on the second floor, the check-in desk a barlike counter usually deserted. When he arrived, he parked the car on a side street and carried his shoulder bag past the jewelers and restaurants and *macellerie*. The entrance of the hotel was inconspicuous and he walked by it twice, once in either direction, until he realized that the door opening on the narrow stairway was what he sought. Finding no one on duty, he sat in a sprung couch in the lobby. The rooms on the floor above faced the railing and he could look up at a filthy skylight. Others might come this way in hope of sun but the natives were more concerned to keep out of it. Half an hour went by and no clerk appeared. He left his bag and went down to street level, looked in at the barbershop next door and said the words he had rehearsed. *"Dove la persona del'albergo?"* It got their attention, however mystified. He stepped onto the sidewalk and pointed at the open door of the hotel. *"Vorrei avere una camera."*

He repeated these serviceable sentences three times, to the growing amusement of the barber and a toothless old man who sat sucking on a cigarette. It was the old man who, suddenly agitated, pointed beyond Webster and shouted, *"Signora, signore, per favore."*

The woman, gray-haired, gray skirt, gray sweater, her stockings fallen to her ankles like struck flags, led him up the stairs with an accompaniment of sighs and groans. How many nights? Several, he wasn't sure. How much? The sum she mentioned was ludicrously low, equivalent to ten dollars. The thought of a nap decided him. When he took out his passport, she glanced at it and pushed it back to him. He had not come to the Ritz.

The room itself was spare and cell-like, a high ceiling, a narrow bed with a feeble reading lamp, a small table, an armoire. He had to step up to the bathroom where an unfrosted window looked into a window in the next building perhaps three feet away. The shower was a metal booth in which he felt like a sentry on duty. He stood at painful attention. There was no way to dodge the alternately hot and cold water. He had not bathed since getting off the freighter. When he stepped out of the shower he heard people talking in the open window across the areaway. He felt neither shame nor defiance. A naked sixty-one-year-old man is a phenomenon, not a scandal, certainly not a concupiscible object. He put on shorts and lay on the bed and looked up at the ceiling feeling, as he had for six weeks now, posthumous.

He felt no regret. He had told Ober he was retired from the human race, a *façon de parler* taken up by the tramp, *mon semblable, mon frère.* How horrible to see a man with whom he had quarreled only hours before hanging dead in his barn, a man at whom he had fired a deer rifle. My God, how easily he might have hit Ober. His aim was erratic at best when he hunted in the woods north of the farm. *Had* he hit Ober? The thought was irrational. A man who is shot does not then go hang himself. He brought a stepladder and sawed through the rope from which Ober was suspended. The body dropped to the concrete floor, teetered briefly on its feet and then fell face forward. It was good not to have to look at the distorted purplish countenance.

Before doing anything with Ober's remains, he stood in the dusty barn wondering how the man could have done it. Drunk, of course, and one does mad and unpredictable things when drunk, as Webster well knew, but any harm that had come his way intoxicated had been accidental, due to his impaired faculties. He would never have deliberately harmed himself and the drunker he was the more incapable of it he would have been. He hunkered down and turned the body over, something surprisingly difficult to do. The term "dead weight" had never been so meaningful.

Where was Ober now? Looking at the shaded face of death, Webster reviewed his supposed beliefs. God made me to know and love him in this world and to enjoy happiness with him forever in the next. Happiness or its opposite. Was Ober in the next world, his particular judgment behind him, all eternity ahead? These theological thoughts produced a kind of envy. Whatever lay beyond, Ober was at last free of this world through which he had made his pointless way into his seventh decade. Webster had heard much of the man's life, but only as a series of episodes, a tale told by an idiot. If Ober had killed himself ten years ago, twenty, what would he have missed, considering it in retrospect, that is? Of course the sense that the future will be different from the past dies hard. While there is life there is hype. If he himself lay dead on the dirty floor of the barn, would he be deprived of any future worth having?

After fifteen minutes, Webster let himself out of the barn and went to the house for whiskey. He had decided to wake his late friend properly. On the way across the yard to the house he felt furtive. What would anyone who showed up and found him with a dead body think? In the house he looked at the phone and imagined calling the village to report what had happened. How would he put it? I've found a tramp hanging in my barn? He could let it be understood that he had never seen the man before but that might be unwise. Despite the distance of the neighbors, the sound of his carousing with Ober might have carried. Besides, there was the mess created last night, not least the broken window in the back door. He did not relish the thought of telling the truth, that he had been Ober's host for over a week, but no more did he want to lie. It was a time when he wished he had made a greater effort to be on good terms with the villagers and his neighbors. They regarded him with suspicion and he in turn regarded them with an indifference verging on contempt. He put it off and sauntered back to the barn for the benefit of possible witnesses and, inside again, pulled the door closed and dropped the crossbar into place.

There was a workbench at one side of the barn that had fallen into desuetude under Webster's ownership. The only making that interested him he did at a desk. Now he sat on a high stool with his back to the bench, carefully poured three ounces into the glass and lifted it in a toast.

"I had not thought death had undone so many."

Ober had known the line but whether from Eliot or Dante was never clear. He seemed genuinely unsure of the source or occasion of the snippets of learning that surprisingly studded his speech. Was he a reader? Had he simply remembered what he heard? Think of the unequal furnishing of human minds. What rattled around in the heads of the villagers? Of the enormously fat man who sold him booze, reluctantly taking his attention from the black-and-white TV that was his link with the wider world. Did the producers of game shows realize their audience included yokels like the Waverly liquor dealer? The local priest had an education of sorts, but that had been long long ago and he now seemed indistinguishable from his fellow villagers. He read his breviary, he said the prayers of the Mass, he preached, he could not be called illiterate, but the common human fate in rural Wisconsin was to become one-third earth, one-third animal and act as humanly as you could with what was left. He picked up his clinking paper bag, feeling that he was a member of another species, and went back to his study to get smashed. Imagine explaining to the liquor dealer what had happened to Ober.

Envy gave way to resentment as the alcoholic content of his blood rose. What a goddam messy thing suicide is, leaving yourself as refuse for others to clear up. It had been the same with Maternowski, whose sweet-and-sour sonnets lingered in the mind. Worse. Jumping from a hotel window into the traffic on Wacker Drive. Banged the hell out of two cars, tied up traffic for half an hour, some portion of him getting washed into the drains by fire hoses. A suicide should exit with grace.

"I can't imagine killing myself," Aran said, but he could imagine killing her. It was already over between them. He talked with her only because there was no one else, and the news of Maternowski's death had made talking imperative.

"If I do, I guarantee you it won't be like that. The best way would be so no one would ever really know for sure."

He babbled on about B. Traven and Ambrose Bierce whose disappearances had intrigued many for years, the better part of a century in Bierce's case. For a long time there had been the possibility that he would walk out of Mexico alive, be found to have been a prisoner of Pancho Villa, or simply to have been thumbing his nose at the world. But a time came when that was not only improbable but impossible. He would have had to be a hundred. So the mystery remained.

The clutter of his writer's head was unleashed by the drink, he sat there feeling pity for himself and a kind of sorrow for Ober. Unbidden came thoughts of prep school, a basement classroom, its window sill flush with a verdant springtime courtyard, Virgil, Book Six of the *Aeneid*. Dido. *Agnosco veteris vestigia flammae*, Aeneas had murmured looking landward from his departing ship and seeing the great funeral pyre on which the body of the abandoned Dido was immolated.

An hour later he was drunkenly dragging from the woods fallen branches of any size he could manage, adding them to the massive stack in the open field.

2

PHILIP KNIGHT had moved to Rye after having been mugged once too often in Manhattan, leaving the city to the beasts of prey that prowled its parks and avenues and to the excessively rich who could afford what it took to survive in the jungle. Instead of offices on Third at enormous rent, he now had ads in the *Yellow Pages* of five large cities, a toll-free number. Expenses dropped, income rose. If he had known of this earlier he would have left even a peaceful Manhattan for the life he and his brother Roger lived in Rye.

Roger was three hundred pounds of blubber and an IQ of 160. More or less. It had been years since he agreed to play laboratory animal for social scientists interested in the inordinately gifted. When he was young and trim, prior to the discovery of his genius, Roger had joined the navy. He made it through boot camp despite his inability to swim— he was putting on weight and floated to qualification—but his awkwardness, his limited attention span, threatened his survival in the service. As had been the case in school up to this point, Roger was suspected of being retarded. It never occurred to others, Philip included, that Roger was stupefied by the stupidity of those around him. While his fate was being decided, Roger was assigned to a casual company. After morning muster he marched the ailing to sick bay and then repaired to the base library where he proceeded to read his way through its modest collection. This was noticed. A thoughtful ensign had Roger subjected to a battery of tests. Thus was the truth discovered. The tests were given twice because of the improbability of the first results. If he had had more muscular coordination, Roger would have been transferred to Annapolis. But the navy had no use for him. He was discharged, admitted to Princeton, and two years later was awarded a doctorate of philosophy for a ten-page paper on the work of Saul Kripke.

This apparent triumph turned into real tragedy when it became clear that Roger was unemployable. He spent two years at the Institute for Advanced Study but he was unclubbable even in that eccentric milieu. Roger nursed the improbable dream of tutoring undergraduates in philosophy but his idea of what everybody already knew was completely unrealistic. He began to eat. He grew very fat. His ungovernable appetite rather than his increasing girth caused him pain. He had become a Catholic despite the efforts of a Princeton chaplain to convince him of the reasonableness of belief.

"The Church is undergoing radical change," the priest assured Roger.

Roger looked at him.

"Since the Council, fresh air has come in through the windows opened by John XXIII."

Roger sat patiently while the agitated cleric spoke of the wonders to come, women's ordination, the repeal of the moral law, democratic election of pastors, every man his own priest.

"Father, I want to be baptized."

The priest beamed at what he took to be the success of his proselytizing. With the saving waters still wet on his head, Roger advised the priest that he was completely confused about Vatican II, that he should read the journal of Pope John XXIII and then go through the Acta of the Council of Trent. Roger had not come into the Church to be told it was undergoing radical change. Of course he did not believe that for a minute. He believed, in the words of the Act of Faith, "everything the holy Catholic church teaches."

Philip was puzzled by this development. When their parents had been killed in an automobile accident and the care of Roger devolved on him, Philip felt angry with a cosmos that could do such things to him and if that qualified as a religious sentiment it had been his only one. But every Sunday he pushed and pulled and tugged Roger into the van and drove him off to Mass. He began on the Sunday papers while he waited. Roger might just as well be retarded after all. Philip had long since given up hope that this was a temporary task, that Roger would grow up, get a job, go off and fend for himself. It would never happen. He had come to hope it would not. Living with Roger was unfailingly interesting.

Roger spent much of the day at his computer, in contact via his modem with research libraries around the world. He was engaged in E-mail correspondence with the wisest in every field that interested him. But it was his childlike innocence that charmed Philip. If anything, Roger was apologetic for his ability to grasp easily what most found wholly unintelligible. And Roger was always a help when an interesting call came in on the toll-free number.

"Does the name Howard Webster mean anything to you, Roger?"

He spun in the extra-large chair and faced Philip. "Yes."

"Who is he?"

"Who was he. A poet of extraordinary power before drink dulled his mind. His first collection was called A *Golden Thigh*, invoking the story told about Pythagoras, of course. I read it in San Diego." The small eyes disappeared as he closed them in thought.

> She pivots on a pretty foot
> Cornering her liquid eyes,
> A turbanned girl now caught
> In pigment. So I surprise
> This moment into words, stop it,
> Zeno's arrow, motionless.
> The read words move with the reader's eye
> As under the wheel the road speeds past—
> But I shall love you till I die.

Roger was waiting for a reaction but Philip merely inclined his head in an ambiguous way.

"He called it '*Panta rei.*' Heraclitus as well as Zeno and Pythagoras. Yet there is no evidence he ever studied philosophy."

"His daughter wants me to come to Milwaukee."

"Of course there was a daughter. One. There were three wives. He was a Catholic, you know. Of a sort."

"It's not my usual cup of tea."

"You must give him a chance. His work is quite traditional in form. He belonged, more or less, to what were called the new metaphysical poets."

"I meant her request."

Felicia Webster Leamon had spent much of the phone call suggesting there was no need for it. She found it difficult to put into words exactly what she wanted. Could he drop by? She was surprised to learn he was not in Milwaukee, but far from putting her off, it seemed to give her resolve. Listening as she spoke rapidly and none too intelligibly about the Webster Foundation, Philip was consigning the call to the category into which the vast majority of inquiries were put. Uninteresting. Not his sort of thing. Once it had been suspicious spouses wanting to know if a wife or husband was unfaithful; now it was prudent young ladies who wanted the medical history of a prospective fiancé. It was Philip Knight's experience that such facts as he could scare up never solved a problem of human trust. How could it ever again be the same between two people after one has spied upon the other? Alas, spouses were sometimes unfaithful and prospective husbands health risks. At least the call from Milwaukee did not fit these humdrum categories. He had told Mrs. Leamon he would call back within the hour. When he asked Roger about Howard Webster he had not expected such enthusiasm.

"What does she want us to do?"

Us? "That's unclear. She has apprehensions about a foundation that was set up . . ."

"And archives. Did she mention the archives?" Roger had read with interest of the conversion of Webster's Wisconsin farm into the repository of his papers. "That is where he died."

"I see."

"It was suicide of the most flamboyant kind. He set himself on fire. Built a huge bonfire and climbed on top of it and struck a match."

"My God!"

"The first interpretation was despair. He hadn't published anything for years, but after his death . . . She mentioned the archives?"

But Roger seemed to know all about the papers of Howard Webster already. It was some relief to learn that Webster was indeed a special interest. The thought that Roger might respond with equal enthusiasm and knowledge to the mention of any obscure poet would have stretched even Philip's credulity.

The upshot was that he called Felicia Webster Leamon

and suggested they talk when he was in Milwaukee the following week. He had resolved not to lie but in the end he did, telling her that he would be in Chicago in any case and could run up to Milwaukee to discuss her concerns with her. No need to mention Roger. He would be shock enough when she saw him. It took time for people to discern beneath the avoirdupois the amiable genius Roger was.

"I won't fly," Roger said.

"We'll drive."

Far better to be in control of their destiny when he traveled with Roger. Besides, Roger could not fit into a tourist class seat, so flying with him was expensive, when he could be persuaded to board the plane. Others found the sight of a grown obese man trembling like a child as he was strapped into his seat comic, but Philip understood. Their parents had perished in an accident and Roger, like many intelligent people, had a compensatory streak of superstition. The prospect of a cross-country jaunt in the van which had been remodeled to accommodate him made Roger exuberant.

"I'll read another poem of Webster's to you."

"Later."

3

WEBSTER STAYED three months in Sant'Antioco, then took
the ferry from Cagliari to Palermo, and drove his rented car
southward to Agrigento where he found a hotel named after
Pirandello. His window faced the sea. He spent his mornings
at his table, looking up from the blank sheet before him to
see the impossible blue of water and sky. It had been thus
in Sant'Antioco as well. Now that he was dead, there seemed
no reason to write, or nothing to write about. He thought
of his oeuvre as standing complete upon the shelf, its author
gone, nothing new to be added now. What did it amount
to, all in all? Not much, and yet he'd had his moments, not
merely a line or two, but whole poems. How many? A
dozen? No, not so much. He would not count the competent, the merely good, only what deserved to last and be
read. He settled on seven. If those seven poems represented
him in an anthology he felt that he would last.

But what did lasting mean except that his poems would
be read by resentful undergraduates? How many readers does

it take to ensure immortality? Immortality whether of the literary kind or of the kind presumably being enjoyed or suffered by Ober seemed part of the Mediterranean landscape, as palpable as sand and rock. He drove out to see the ruins of the Greek theater. Sophocles had premiered a play here. Sophocles would be read as long as there are readers, yet the dramatist could not possibly have imagined the world into which his plays had survived.

Webster picked up his pen and wrote carefully the Greek alphabet in lower case. Twenty-four letters and to his surprise he remembered them all. The years at Murray Hall had been the most formative of his life, from age thirteen to seventeen, years during which he had been taught Latin and Greek as well as French, where reading American and English literature was an extracurricular joy, where the only science course he took was laughably inane. The one thing he remembered from it was the information that a then popular liquid dentifrice achieved its effect by eating enamel from the teeth. How much more would he have remembered if it had been a good course? How much did he remember of other courses, the Greek alphabet aside? How much French did he remember? Once he had actually written poems in French, teased by Eliot's example. He had not published them but neither had he thrown them away. Would they be found now and commented on?

He told himself he did not care what the reaction to his going was. In Chicago he had read of his fiery suicide, skimming the story, assured that the ruse had worked. He had slipped the ring Aran had given him onto the dead finger of Ober but there was no mention of this in the story. But why should anyone doubt that the bones and ashes discovered in the wood ashes were his? When he boarded the freighter he paid his passage from the twenty thousand dollars he had realized from the sale of the government savings bonds that had accumulated during his teaching years. In Sicily he was still living on that twenty thousand. How long would it last? When it was gone he would be poor indeed, and what would he do then?

He did not choose to think about it. With no future he could live in the moment and that is what he would do. Let the future take care of itself. He celebrated the anniversary of his death in Siracusa. It was the feast of a local saint and he followed the procession with as much devotion as curiosity, the statue of the saint swaying above the crowd as it was carried on the shoulders of eight sweating men gotten up in a quasi-military uniform. There was one brass band at the head of the procession and another bringing up the rear, just behind the bishop. Webster thought of himself as in Limbo, the place reserved for children who die unbaptized and for good pagans. He was not dead enough to qualify for any other place in the divine comedy. From time to time he sat in cool, gaudy churches and remembered what it was like to believe. Ah, the zeal he had felt when he became a Catholic. Those first years he had gone to daily Mass, early in the morning, the liturgy still Latin then. There had been an odd snobbery in his conversion. Shifting his weight to take the pressure from his knees, he thought of himself as the companion of Dante and Chaucer, of Erasmus and More as well as of Graham Greene, Chesterton, Waugh. Belloc too. Especially Belloc. He loved Belloc. *Do you remember an inn, Miranda, do you remember an inn?* But Belloc had wanted to be a don even more than he had wanted to be a poet. In the end he wrote for his bread, pouring out essays and doggerel and history and novels, anything that was wanted. What if he had been able to do nothing but write poetry?

He would have done nothing. Webster's own good stuff had been written when he didn't have the time, under adverse circumstances, not seeming any better than anything else he had written, certainly not up to what he hoped eventually to write. When he settled down on the farm under optimum conditions, when there were few distractions from his writing, when at last he could do the work he was destined to do, he came to fear his best work was already behind him. He had fought that fear with booze and quarrels with women when he wasn't trying to screw their ears off. Of course he had continued to hope that with time he would write again.

He had been given time and all he had managed to do of any substance was the fictional journal he had dashed off while Ober was in the house. That too would be there to be paged through by anyone interested in his stuff.

It came to seem an affectation to think that he was remembered. He had seen too many reputations plunge with the death of the poet. Maybe his funeral pyre would win him attention as Berryman's dive off the bridge in Minneapolis had for him. He was swallowed up by the Mississippi but it might have been a publicity stunt. When Webster pushed the body of Ober out to the stacked wood his only thought had been that this corpse was his ticket out of the impasse his life had become.

He drove back to Agrigento and up to Palermo. He wanted to be back in Sant'Antioco. He abandoned the rented car in a parking lot near the ferry dock. He could take the train from Cagliari. The woman in his hotel did not recognize him or if she did gave no sign of it. But he was given the very same room as before. He had thought of asking for it, but decided to let fate decide. It was May and in the yellow church near the sea half a churchful of women said the rosary before the afternoon Mass. The church was new, the windows clear, sun spilled all over the pews. It did not seem an Italian church at all.

A week after he returned to Sant'Antioco he went into the barbershop next to the hotel. His last haircut had been in Siracusa, three months before. For the first time in his life he looked like a poet. The barber handed him an American magazine after tying the cloth around his neck. His face was on the cover. The story sang the praises of Howard Webster whose life had ended so tragically in Wisconsin. Webster read with disbelief the description of himself as among the perhaps two or three genuine poetic talents of the past half century in America. But even more astounding was the account of his novella *The Leaden Echo*. The reference was to the fictional journal he had written during those last days when Ober was with him.

The barber continued busily clipping while he read but Webster was still too stunned to care when he saw the clipped, talced, oiled self that looked back at him from the mirror. Neither before nor after the tonsorial treatment did he resemble the poet in the magazine.

4

THEY TOOK I-80 through Pennsylvania, then the Ohio Turnpike and Indiana Toll Road, spending a night in Youngstown and another in Chicago before heading north for Milwaukee. Roger, ensconced in a swivel chair, worked on his laptop, surely a misnomer in his case, he having no lap for the computer to rest upon. He was working on Bell's Theorem, whatever that was, and for hours he might have been in his workroom in Rye for all he noticed of the countryside. But when he did turn off the computer he marveled at the flatland through which they passed. Great trucks roared by on either side of them, the commerce of the nation wheeling along. The golden dome of Notre Dame came and went and soon they were in the unbreathable atmosphere of Gary. Perhaps allowing the Japanese to become steelmakers for the world was a subtle kind of revenge. Roger's thought. Phil had both hands on the wheel and a wary eye out for Illinois drivers as they swept through Chicago's loop.

Felicia Leamon had offered to get them hotel rooms in

Milwaukee, but Phil wanted to see and hear more before he committed himself. As far as Roger was concerned, they were at the disposal, if not yet in the employ, of Felicia. Roger had refreshed his memory on the career and fiery end of Howard Webster.

"He wrote little on others' poetry but there is an essay on Hopkins's poem " 'That Nature Is a Heraclitean Fire.' ' "

"No kidding."

"Again, the philosophical predilection." Roger dipped into a bag and took out one of the Big Macs he had bought at the last oasis. The first oasis on the trip had sent Roger into a spiel about the Arab influence in Western culture—algebra, our numbering system, now oasis.

"Don't forget Camel cigarettes."

" 'Mosques rise over the old cities of Christendom. White founts falling in the courts of the sun. . . .' " Roger intoned. "Lepanto may have been only a battle, not the war."

Philip failed to see the attraction Howard Webster held for Roger. The poet sounded like a drearily familiar phenomenon, the aging bard playing to student audiences, pinching coeds, failing to grow up, stopping even the production of poems some years before his death, then bringing his life to a close in a pathetic bid for attention. But Roger likened it to Shelley's body being burnt on the Ligurian coast. He could not speak prose five consecutive minutes when speaking of Webster, breaking into verse, Webster's or another's.

"Philip, it is uncanny how his writings comment on his life."

Roger had read *The Leaden Echo* aloud through Pennsylvania and much of Ohio, relishing it, pausing from time to time as if in deference to Philip's supposed silent transports. Roger said it might have been a nonfiction account of the poet's last days.

"Only the wrong one dies."

"Of course there is only one character, the narrator. The visitor is himself, reified by liquor, the person he has become appearing to him with all its sins upon its head, the inescapable self-judgment on Howard Webster." Half a minute's pause. "The story is unclear as to whether he retained his religious faith. The suicide tells against that, perhaps."

They stayed in a motel west of the city—it was always easier getting Roger into and out of a unit when they could pull the van to the very door—and after showering and a nap, Philip went alone to speak with Felicia.

What should the daughter of a poet look like? Felicia was slim, seemed taller than she was and had large lidded eyes and a prominent nose. Striking rather than beautiful, but very striking.

"I must have sounded incoherent on the phone, Mr. Knight. You realize I had no idea I was speaking to someone clear across the country. As it turns out, that is best. Milwaukee is in many ways a small town and anything having to do with my father is likely to attract the curious."

"It was no trouble to come up from Chicago."

She ignored this cautionary note. "The problem is twofold. One is merely legal and I don't imagine you or anyone else can help me much with that. The other is more difficult to describe."

The legal problems, he had gathered from their phone conversations, concerned the foundation that had been set up to dispense the posthumous proceeds from her father's writing. Philip could easily imagine that the poet's daughter would want to have veto power over what the officers of the foundation decided to do. And he could also imagine she could be a pain in the neck about it.

"A young man named Albert Clinton was hired as executive director of the foundation. That meant he was to take up residence at the farm, catalogue my father's papers, be custodian and archivist. He and his wife have moved to Madison."

"Did he resign?" If he had followed his own instincts he would not have permitted Felicia's inquiry go beyond a first telephone conversation. It was because of Roger that he had come this far. And for what? To hear that there was internal dissension in the foundation and that there was a problem with an employee as well?

"Mrs. Leamon, I am a private investigator. Nothing you've said seems to require my particular competence."

"I think there are papers missing."

"Why do you think so?"

"Have you heard of *The Leaden Echo*?"

"Yes."

"Clinton discovered that. Royalties from it account for a good deal of the endowment of the foundation. Its publication history makes the manuscript even more valuable than it otherwise would have been. Clinton has reported the manuscript missing."

"Reported to whom?"

"Me. This is the chief reason I called you, but I wanted to tell you face-to-face. And of course in confidence. Clinton called to tell me the manuscript was missing in the same conversation in which he was in effect telling me that he and his wife had moved to Madison."

She threw up her hands and a waiter leapt to what he took to be her signal. She dismissed him with practiced authority. They had met in a tearoom on the top floor of a local department store. Philip was one of half a dozen males in a sea of women. Mention of the missing manuscript made this trip less pointless.

"What kind of security is there at the farm?"

"With Clinton and Jane in Madison? That's a good question. There are deadbolt locks on the outer doors but there are half a dozen ways into the house. Basement windows, the windows in the library. There is an alarm system but it does not inform the village police. Not that it would make much difference if it did. The safety of the papers was predicated on the presence on the property of Clinton the custodian."

She told him with manifest irritation that Clinton had argued that there was no formal requirement that he actually live on the farm. He commuted from Madison, claimed to be at his desk five days a week and rejected her suggestion that he had been delinquent.

"That's Jane, of course. His wife. I was suspicious of her girlish enthusiasm when he took the job. She is very likely a manic depressive and was in one of her high moods. I know she forced Clinton to move. His devotion to my father's work is genuine and of long duration."

"Do you think he stole the manuscript?"

"Good heavens, no!" She seemed shocked by the suggestion.

"You don't think it was stolen?"

"It's missing, certainly. Clinton is the one who told me it was."

"So he couldn't have taken it?"

"Why would he tell me?"

"You know him. I don't."

"I suppose he could have, I never thought of it. It just doesn't fit his attitude toward the papers."

Her views of Clinton were certainly mixed. On the one hand she regarded his move from the farm to Madison as a base betrayal. And however much she blamed the custodian's wife for the move, it was unclear that they didn't have the right to do it. Being in residence may have been her understanding when she hired him, but she admitted it had not been written down. On the other hand, she clearly could not bring herself to think that Clinton had taken the manuscript he reported missing.

"He couldn't have meant mislaid?"

"He had turned the house upside down before calling me."

"So it was stolen."

"That's what I want you to find out. I can't make a public fuss about it. For personal reasons as well as others."

"You want it recovered?"

"Exactly."

Of course there would be a traffic in manuscripts and other memorabilia of authors, but as with works of art the spoor of such illegal transactions would not be easy to follow. This might have dissuaded Philip if he had shared Felicia's reluctance to assume that Clinton had something to do with the missing manuscript. Reporting it could have been shrewd calculation rather than an index of innocence.

"I'll take you to the farm," she offered when he had accepted the assignment to find the missing manuscript.

"I think it will be better if I just drop by. It is open to the public, isn't it?"

"You don't want Clinton to know I've hired you?"

Thank God it had come up. Clearly he could not assume things with Mrs. Leamon. But her naiveté did underscore her belief in Clinton's innocence. She had sat back and was looking at him with narrowed eyes.

"No, I don't think he would know you're a detective."

Not with Roger along, he wouldn't. However many people had visited the shrine to Howard Webster, Philip doubted that any more dedicated fan than Roger had been there.

5

THE ISSUE of the magazine was nearly a year old when Webster read it. Never had he felt so dead, so posthumous, as when he read the adulatory account of his career, all the verbs in the past tense. The fame and praise he had wanted for years and, if this article was right, had deserved all along, were heaped upon him dead. Nor was the article a solitary salute. He read with amazement of the publication of the fictionalized account he had written of Ober's last days. The list of best-sellers in the magazine confirmed the book's success. The demotic touch had always eluded him in life, but what was called his novella had sold several hundred thousand copies at the time the magazine story was written. Had its success continued? Its success would have been monetary as well as critical. Money was involved, a great deal of money. Howard Webster realized that, since his death, he had become a rich man.

He tipped the barber five thousand lire and took the magazine with him when he went out onto the shaded walk. He looked now one way, now the other, and either way there was light at the end of the tunnel. The direction he took led toward the narrow stretch of water separating the smaller island from the larger, Sant'Antioco from Sardinia. He might have been moving toward the wealth and prestige that were now his but as he walked he began to think of the complications of his position.

For over a year, he had been considered dead, which meant that the illusion he had sought to create when he burned Ober's body had occurred. At the time he had wanted to escape from the shambles of his life, from the depressing sense of having lived in vain. Ober's cremation had been his purgation. Once at sea on the freighter with the taste of salt spray in his mouth he had felt cleansed of his past, anonymous, everyman bound for nowhere. And although he was disturbed now by the incredible news he had just read there was no doubt that during his stay in Sardinia and Sicily he had felt born again, almost in a religious sense. How often had he sat in churches in the half hope that faith would return and he could believe that the flickering sanctuary light signaled the sacramental presence of Jesus.

Jesus. In Siracusa he had formed the thought of going to Israel, the Holy Land, and visiting the places that had marked the life of Christ. Perhaps there where those events, shrouded in pious legend and ardent faith, had happened, he would respond again to the incredible claim that an obscure Galilean had been God incarnate. But he dared not risk Israeli security. Any tourist who was in effect carrying the passport of a dead man would attract attention. Was there a list of the deceased holders of passports? He thought of going to Rome, not now but later, as a fallback position. Meanwhile he had settled for Sardinian churches but nothing had happened.

How cheaply he had lived, husbanding the money he had realized from cashing his government savings bonds. Had

that transaction aroused any curiosity? Not if the article he
had just read and would read again and again was any indication. No doubt was cast on the identity of the body that had
burned on that pyre.

Felicia. He had hurried past mentions of his daughter in
the newsmagazine story, not wanting to dwell on the fact
that he had let her think he was dead. What did it matter
if for all practical purposes he was dead? Only now, when
resurrection had its attractions, did the effect of his reappear-
ance on Felicia present problems.

How long had it been since they had seen one another?
She had visited him at the farm, once with her husband,
several times alone, duty calls that had been uncomfortable
for both of them. After she was gone he would be besieged
by memories of her as a child and this brought back the
time before his personal life had become confused with his
persona as a poet. His first poems had been written without
any consciousness of himself as different from the rest of
men. If he had felt any conflict between his literary ambitions and his commitment to his wife and child he could
not recall them. All that had come later. The more he lived
like a poet the less poetry he had written. Finally he was
swallowed up in his persona and stopped writing altogether.
Felicia's visits contributed mightily to his sense of having
wasted his life. How could he show up now, more than a
year and a half after his supposed death, and expect anything
but her horrified rejection? Before he had emerged from the
shadowy tunnel that was the main street of Sant'Antioco he
had decided he could not return to the land of the living.

He took a bus north from Cagliari, stopping at Bosa where
he found a hotel from which he could look westward and
seaward. His balcony had room for one folding chair and for
a full day he sat in it, altering its angle so that he always had
the sun. It was too hot to sleep and uncomfortable enough to
make consecutive thought impossible. He did not want to

think. He wanted the mindless existence that had been his for over a year, no past, no future, just the day in which he lived. But that had been effortless when it was a true description of his existence. Now it was an affectation. At five in the afternoon, he went inside, pulled the blinds and lay on the bed. The walls were chalk-white plaster, smooth as a geometrical plane. The blinds made a sunny ladder that conformed itself to the table, then climbed up the wall. On the ceiling a light trembled, a reflection from some window or bit of glass outside. He felt laid out for burial. Howard Webster, poet.

Could he write poetry still? In his posthumous state there had been no incentive to do what he had done in life. Once he bought a paperback of Leopardi's poems and whispered them over to himself, enjoying the sound and rhythms, only imperfectly understanding them. What an odd thing poetry is, odd arrangements of words on the page, melodies sounding in the head, the meaning coming only afterward if at all. When he thought of the hours, days, years, he had devoted to this activity, it seemed a double waste. What did it matter whether one was good or bad at such an essentially silly activity?

Now lying in his bed, no longer resisting the effect of that article, feeling unjustly dealt with because he could not come forward and accept in person the accolades of his admirers, he found himself stirred by the need to write. If he should return, as if from the dead, with a collection of new poems, would he not be forgiven, welcomed, feted? Not by Felicia of course. That would be too much to expect.

Before the day was out he tried to write again, a verse letter to his daughter. Unsuccessfully.

6

IN THE village, Philip stopped at a filling station to ask directions to the Webster farm. Roger pushed open the door and managed to get out of the van unaided and the sight of him drew a crowd.

"Did you know the poet?" Roger asked the slack-jawed yokel who was putting gas in the tank. The boy's expression suggested he was often the butt of jokes and did not propose to lay himself open to another.

"Howard Webster," Philip said.

The boy wiped his hand on the leg of his overalls and extended it. "Wilmer."

Phil shook the soiled hand, there seemed no way to avoid it. "My name is Philip Knight."

The boy withdrew his hand and looked narrowly at Philip. Fooled again.

Philip turned to the two men who had sidled up and were pretending not to notice the strangers who had arrived in their midst.

"Does either of you know of a farm that was bought by a man named Webster?"

"Bates place."

"Two miles out of town," the other added, dipping a shoulder directionally.

"Thanks."

"He's dead, you know."

"Yes."

"Webster, not Bates. Bates is dead too."

"I see."

"Alvin Bates is still alive."

"We're interested in Webster."

"He's dead."

"I realize that. He was a great writer."

The mouth of one went up, that of the other down, tragic and comic masks. Philip thanked them for their help and returned to where Roger was in animated conversation with the gas attendant.

Roger was explaining how long it took petroleum to form and the boy insisted that the tanker had delivered this gas just a week ago. It was not in Roger's nature to leave things at such an impasse, but Philip took his elbow and steered him toward the van. When they were rolling out of the village—speed limit 20—Philip said, "One thing is sure, Webster didn't move here for the company."

"One reads that television has overcome the sharp distinction between the urban and rural."

"One reads wrong."

"Amen."

From the road the farm and house were modest enough and the impression did not change as Philip picked his way up the rutted drive. To hear that a poet has retired to a farm suggests a country estate, verdant surroundings, natural beauty. On this gray day the smell that rose from the muddy fields was fetid, little greenness relieved the shades of gray and black that dominated the landscape. Even the birds seemed evolutionary rejects, their songs unmusical.

"They're crows," Roger said with apparent approval.

Philip came up behind the house where a barn much like that described in *The Leaden Echo* came into view. There was an ancient Japanese car parked with its nose against the barn door. By the time they got out of the van, a young man appeared on the back porch, adjusting his glasses nervously.

"Welcome to the Webster Archives," he cried.

7

MORNINGS HE sat for hours at his desk, paper before him, pen in hand, but the only things he wrote were remembered verses of his own. That had seemed a way to prime the pump, to stir his imagination, to begin again. At the outset he felt almost solemn seated at the desk, remembering the exalted praise of the newsmagazine story. He had read it many times now and the impact did not lessen. It seemed the vindication of his life's work. He had set out to be a poet and now by common acknowledgment he was numbered among the top half-dozen poets of his generation, some ranked him first.

It was a heady notion after the ambiguous years when it was far easier to think he had failed. Failed twice, if Yeats was right.

> The intellect of man is forced to choose
> Perfection of the life or of the work
> And if the latter must refuse
> A heavenly mansion, raging in the dark.

Parnassus or hell? It seemed he had missed the one and deserved the other. He could not forget how he had failed Felicia. It was too late to make up to his first two wives for his treatment of them, and of course he was still Catholic enough to think of only his first wife as real. One night he dreamed of Aran and for half a morning missed her, but other memories replaced the pleasant ones. It was not to see her again that he was tempted to rise from the dead. If he thought there was any realistic chance of a reconciliation with Felicia . . .

But what kept him in Sardinia, trying not to think of how long he could survive on the cash he had, was the thought that his literary career now had a beginning, a middle and an end, and it would be fatal to reopen it. This conviction was helped by his inability to write any new poetry.

In late summer in a bookstore in Sassari he came upon an Italian translation of *The Leaden Echo. Dissonanza.* His first impulse was to cry out, to hold up the book and announce that he was its author. But he controlled himself, bought a copy and walked to a park where on a bench he opened the book.

At first he thought it was the translation. He read the opening paragraphs and then, frowning, began to page through the book. He read the ending slowly, trying to imagine the English. He went back to the beginning and began to read. The thing to do was read it carefully, not just flip around in it. After several pages he closed the book. It was all he could do not to throw it in a receptacle for trash. The legend at the beginning of the book was clear. The translation was of the American edition, arrangements having been made with the Boswell Press. It was not the translation that was at fault. The book was not his. The novella that had sold a million copies and had made his posthumous name was not the manuscript he had left.

1
PART THREE

IN THE airport limo—a bus—from O'Hare, a child cried continuously, its young mother seemingly unperturbed by the wailing. Frank, unable to concentrate on anything else, concentrated on the crying—its pitch and range, its different rhythms, cries of apparent pain giving way to uncontrollable sobbing. Why didn't some woman on the goddam bus get up and help the mother, hold the kid, stop the endless bawling? Several times he himself stirred, intending to lurch up the aisle and offer to hold the baby.

It angered him that he was so bothered by that crying. He thought of himself as a man who loved children, who beamed with approval on the young who reproduced themselves. He was sure that the only reason they had only two children was that Felicia was unwilling but even at that she was an improvement over his first wife. Imagine Marge having one, let alone several. Keeping her figure became an obsession with her and bouts of starving alternated with frenzied stuffing. Once after two weeks of a punitive diet, she had done away with a two pound box of soda crackers, crumbling them in a bowl and pouring milk over them, spooning the mixture into her greedy mouth. He would pay for it, she would compensate with another stretch of starvation and when Marge starved so did he. At least at home. During the day he could pull into fast food places and pig out with impunity. At first it was a relief when Marge left him. Or failed to come back. She went to visit her sister in California and over the phone informed him that she was staying.

"Stay as long as you like."

"I'm not coming back, Frank. Ever."

He thought about it. What a hell of a way to tell him. Was her sister hovering in the background, lending moral support?

"Think it over, Marge. Take your time."

"I have thought it over."

He didn't agree and he didn't disagree. The divorce went through and he met and married Felicia and that was that. Except that, because of the way she had left him, Marge seemed like unfinished business. Which was why from time to time he flew to California to see her.

This visit to Marge had been like the others. She might have been a relative he hadn't seen for a while. They got along well enough, in a distant sort of way. Leave it to her sister Gen to mention the guy Marge was going out with. Frank hadn't liked that at all, not that he had any claim on her. He himself had stayed chaste as a monk after Marge left, but that was because of the pace he led. At night he was dead tired and if he often lay sleepless it was because his head was humming with money-making schemes. He sometimes wondered if it was the low ebb of his sexual aggressiveness that had attracted Felicia. At the time she had seemed more abandoned than he was, her mother dead, a famous father who didn't give a damn for her. Frank had liked Howard Webster a lot better living than dead. Not that they ever saw him, but he had by killing himself turned Felicia into a wealthy woman. A visit to Marge in California was some respite from his altered wife.

Hector had proved more patient than most partners but he was getting fed up too. If his secretary had anything to do with it, Frank would have turned to another source of capital long ago. They were a lot alike, Hector and Frank, both dreaming of a scheme that would pay off in huge amounts. Against all reason, against all experience, Frank plunged on from one glittering possibility to the next. He had enough self-knowledge to see how misbegotten earlier schemes were, but the current one was always an exception, what he had been looking for all along.

The crying baby seemed to be finding new avenues of agony. There had been a lull when hope descended over the darkened bus but then the crying started again and Frank could see the passengers shift under the new onslaught. Wasn't crying always a sign of something, illness, a safety pin undone, pricking the flesh, dirty diapers, something? Surely babies didn't just cry like that. Frank remembered, or thought he remembered, nights when he had paced the floor with one of his children, soothing it, letting Felicia get some sleep. But at the moment Frank felt an unwilling sympathy for the poor wretches one saw on television who had smothered their children, drowned them, beaten them. No doubt they reached a point when they just had to stop the crying. Dreadful thought.

In California he had checked out a dealer in manuscripts, asking who was hot at the moment. No mention of Howard Webster. Finally, Frank asked the man if he had ever heard of Webster. The man pressed the tip of his nose and this seemed to cause his eyes to lift.

"You think I'm an idiot, in this line of work?"

"What does he bring?"

"An autograph, a letter, what?"

"Letters."

"How many?"

"How much?"

"I gotta see them first, of course. You got them with you?"

Frank shook his head. "I wouldn't want to bother you with something insignificant."

"Show me some Webster letters and we'll talk."

The man wouldn't give him a price. Not surprising, when you thought of it, but Frank asked about things on display. Some poet named Robinson Jeffers commanded a fairly good price.

"Man sold me those financed a trip to Europe for him and his wife."

Excursion rate, first class, what? Still, that was some kind of clue. He felt he had enough to mention the possibility to Felicia. It would enable her to recoup some of the confidence she had lost by getting mixed up with that crook Cannon.

"How many of your father's letters do you have?" he asked Felicia the following day.

"None!" But then, remembering Howard Webster's posthumous status, she said, "Why do you ask?"

"You could sell them."

"How much are they worth?"

"A man financed a European trip selling a few letters, first class, with his wife."

"How many letters?"

"I thought you didn't have any."

2

THE AFTERNOON spent showing Roger Knight and his brother through the archives was one of the most enjoyable Clinton had spent in a month. The daily drive back and forth to Madison—following a serpentine country road to where he could pick up the Interstate and dodge among the semis until his turnoff, the last one into Madison—had taken its toll on his psyche. The least they might have done is rent on the north side of the city, as close as possible to the farm, but Jane was not generous in victory and exacted total capitulation. Her objective was to live as close to the campus as possible and indeed she had almost immediately reverted to coed status once they settled in; she was auditing several courses, hanging about the rathskeller, trying desperately to overlook the fact that she was a decade older than the students. But her new enthusiasm got her out of his hair and there was much to be said for that. So he rose at five each morning and was on his way before six. Even on good days the drive took two hours and he made it a rule to be open for business at nine.

Except that business seldom came. There was the occasional phone call, dribs and drabs of mail, but by and large he spent the day in solitude. He indulged in self-pity about this, laying the blame for it on Jane's doorstep, but the truth was he was quite content to have the house and papers to himself. Such visitors as he had were old rivals, anxious to see for themselves the sinecure he had. Wilma Maddox flew into Milwaukee and came on by rented car. She was the doyenne of Webster experts; it was rumored that she had slept with the great man, though this must have been while Webster was drunk. To the sober, Wilma was anything but seductive. The formation of her front teeth made her mouth seem open even when her great lips were closed, she had enough nose for a family of three, such shape as her body had was mercifully concealed behind ankle-length, commodious dresses vaguely Hawaiian in style. For all that, she had striking red hair and knew Webster's work better than anyone else. Clinton called up on the computer the catalogue he was creating and she nodded approval. He let her have free rein in looking through the papers and even let her use Webster's desk.

"I want to stay over and work here again tomorrow."

"Wonderful."

"I suppose there's a hotel in the village."

"You can stay here. I'll be running down to Madison but I'll be back in the morning. You can work on into the night if you'd like. Come, I'll show you your room."

"Howard's?"

"Yes."

"I can find it."

It was the female equivalent of thumping the chest, he supposed. She avoided his eyes, which oddly gave more rather than less credence to the suggestion that it was in that upstairs room that she had surrendered herself to the poet of her dreams.

Later when he reported the manuscript of *The Leaden Echo* missing he had been asked who could possibly have gained access to it and of course he had mentioned Wilma's two day visit and the fact that she had stayed overnight in the house. In fairness he added that she had shown absolutely no curiosity at all about Webster's prose work. She had not asked to see the manuscript and indeed had made a point of saying she had not read the story. It was Webster the poet that interested her.

Levy had come, visibly jealous of Clinton's good luck, but compensating for it by guffawing about the rustic setting.

"I wouldn't last a week here," he said, hands in his back pockets, looking out over the dusty fields to the stand of woods. Chicken hawks circled in the distance and a ribbon of cloud was stretched across the sky.

"Webster loved it."

Levy gave him the fish eye. "He had no choice."

Why argue? Levy would have crawled from Kansas to get this job and they both knew it. "Jane and I live near the campus in Madison."

"I thought living here was part of the job."

"Jane found it lonely."

Levy frowned at this, as if Clinton was holding the position on a false basis. Clinton felt the same way, but he wasn't going to encourage Levy to think so.

In any case, Levy's name too had to be mentioned when Clinton was questioned by Felicia about the missing manuscript. She seemed more concerned to keep the theft quiet than to find the thief, although she had said she would do something about it. It became clear she did not mean to inform the police. The day with Roger Knight had been marred when, late in the afternoon, it emerged that Philip Knight was a private investigator hired by Felicia to find out what had happened to the manuscript of *The Leaden Echo*.

"Philip wasn't sure who Howard Webster was when the

call came," Roger said. "Thank God he mentioned it to me."

"How will he go about finding the manuscript?"

"Don't hurry him," Roger said. "The longer it takes, the better."

It was impossible not to be struck by Roger Knight's enormous size but it was his surprising knowledge of Howard Webster's work and career that impressed Clinton. He would have expected to be telling his two guests the more obvious things about the poet's career but within fifteen minutes he had the uneasy feeling that Roger knew as much about Webster as he did. When five o'clock came, however, he did not, as he had with Wilma, suggest that the Knight brothers spend the night at the farm.

Watching the van feel its way down the rutted drive to the road, Roger sitting in the exact center of the middle seat so as not to imbalance the vehicle, Clinton regretted not having asked them to stay. Never had driving off to Madison at twilight seemed more delinquent to him. He went inside and phoned Jane and told her he was staying the night.

"What on earth for?"

"There are visitors. They want to come back early in the morning."

"What difference does that make? God knows you get up early enough."

"If I stay here I can get a good night's sleep for a change."

"What's that supposed to mean?"

That quickly she was spoiling for a fight. She wouldn't be so touchy if she didn't feel guilty too. On the rare occasions when he had won an argument with Jane he had found it worse than losing. How petty any contention seemed once it was over. Now, hearing the snarl in her voice, he was reminded of what suddenly seemed years of quarreling. In the yard one squirrel chased another, their tails erect and plumelike; the pursued sprang to a tree and circling it went out of sight, swiftly followed by the pursuer. They reappeared in rising spirals until the lead squirrel went out a leafless limb and sprang into space. For a moment there was a furry silhouette and then the animal landed on the very end of a slim branch of a mountain ash. The branch became a swaying metronome as the squirrel consolidated its position and then rested while its pursuer contemplated the wisdom of imitating that daring leap. Of course it did and the wild chase continued. A courtship? It seemed sufficiently pointless and foolhardy.

"Jane, I'm just too damned tired to do that drive now and then again in the morning."

"Are you blaming me?"

"No, Jane, I'm blaming me."

He put the phone gently back into its cradle. Long-distance arguments were more absurd than those conducted face-to-face. He went onto the back porch and stood there ignoring the phone that began to ring before he got to the door. He went down the porch steps, to get away from the sound. The man coming up the drive lifted a hand in greeting as if Clinton might know who he was.

Clinton readied his explanation that the place was closed for the day. Where had the man come from? There was no car in evidence. Walking in an odd gait, his body half turned, bearded chin lifted, beret atop the thick white hair, the man came smiling up to Clinton.

"My name's Ober."

Clinton stepped back involuntarily. No wonder he had had the sense of living something through again. This was the opening scene in *The Leaden Echo* and Ober might be stepping from its pages. If he was a tramp he was a more prosperous one than had visited Howard Webster, chino pants, a black denim jacket, a red turtleneck, the beret. The weathered face was full of sun and the eyes squinted as if secreting thought.

"I spent some time here with Webster before he died."

"How did you get here?"

"The old boy and I had some pretty good sessions. As the whole world knows now, right?"

"You've read *The Leaden Echo?*"

"I've read about it anyway." He looked toward the house. "Webster always had a pot of coffee on."

It was with a sense of inevitability that Clinton invited Ober inside. He might have been conceding to him seigneurial rights that antedated his own. Ober had talked and drunk and fought with Howard Webster whereas Clinton had never seen his literary hero alive. He had been at once too shy and too proud to write Webster and ask if he could come talk with him about the "Baraboo Elegies." He had sent the poet a copy of his dissertation and received what had to be a form letter acknowledging receipt of the copy and saying he looked forward to reading it. But there had been no further letter. Had Webster ever read that painstaking exegesis of what Clinton considered Webster's masterpiece? It seemed unfair that a drifter like Ober should have become an intimate of the poet and even prompted Webster to turn the prolonged visit into prose.

3

THE WEEPING willows still wept along the road on the way to the farm, insects buzzed in the pollen-filled air, the smell of the fields filled his nostrils, but he had no real sense of returning home. This was the road on which a year and half before he had fled the living death his life had become, liberated by Ober's suicide, free to be dead if he chose, and he chose. His going should have been covered with the same silence as his career, perhaps a local flourish, maybe some academic attention to the manner of his leaving this world, but finally silence enclosing who he had been. Discovery of his posthumous fame held ironic pleasure until he learned that the fame was based on an apocryphal novella. The supposedly late poems also belonged to someone else. Better oblivion to this. He returned angry and intent on revenge. And he returned as Ober.

The young man squinting at him as he came up the road had to be the curator of his papers, the discoverer of the supposed novella. He had recognized the name as that of a boring correspondent who had importuned him with inquiries about the "Baraboo Elegies." Such academic attention seemed the kiss of death rather than what he had longed for and he had answered perfunctorily. Clinton had never asked for a personal interview and Webster did not fear recognition now. Besides, after Sardinia, he was a stranger to himself, grizzled, browned, lean. The jacket and chinos were new but manufactured to look old and his sneakers, veterans from the Sardinia sojourn, bore the dust of the road from the village. The beret had been bought in Palermo. Compared to the Ober who had first turned up at the farm, he was dapper, but he had put on the persona from the novella. It seemed fitting that a stranger should welcome him back to his own farm. He glanced at the barn as he followed the curator into the house.

"You're in residence here?"

Clinton's eyes slid away. Webster expected a practiced liar and was surprised at such telegraphing of mendacity. The clerk in the village bus station had told him all the news of the farm. He had not recognized Webster, but then he had always kept away from the village, except for the liquor store. Had the villagers known as much about him as they did about Clinton? When he set out for the farm, he avoided the liquor store, and started out the country road. A van forced him onto the shoulder but for the rest of the way he had the road to himself. Memories of his visits to the village liquor store seemed mythical. In Sardinia he had all but stopped drinking, a glass of wine at meals, perhaps, but mineral water was equally satisfactory. Imagine drinking a single glass of anything in the old days. Dead men don't drink? Sun slanting at him from the west and the dry smell of weeds brought back a forgotten thirst.

"Congratulations on the novella," Webster said, accepting the cup of coffee. Instant coffee. A defect of hospitality there, but then Clinton seemed unsure how to treat him.

"Congratulations?"

"Didn't you discover it?"

"It wasn't hidden. Anyone would have come upon it."

"Anyone in your job?"

"What did you think of the story?"

"How would *you* like to end up as a fictional character?" Webster asked.

"Ober is your real name?" replied Clinton.

"It's the name he knew me by."

"Tell me about your visit here."

"Isn't that what the novella does?"

"Did you know he was writing it?"

Webster tipped his cup and saw himself reflected in the coffee. "He didn't call it a novella."

"Did he show it to you?"

"I'd like to see it again."

Had Clinton written the novella himself? It was certain he had not found in the study what was published as *The Leaden Echo*. "It's missing."

"Missing!"

Clinton nodded quickly, as if rewarding Webster for understanding. "I was going to show it to a visitor and found it wasn't where I'd stored it."

"But who would take it?"

"Webster manuscripts are worth a good deal now."

"Has it turned up?"

"Mrs. Leamon has hired someone to find it. She's Webster's daughter."

His feelings about Felicia were not the remorseful ones that had plagued him on Sant'Antioco. Obviously she had welcomed the role of the dead poet's daughter, setting up the foundation, hiring Clinton. She had taken no money, apparently, but what need did she have for money?

"Do you think they'll find it?"

"I don't know." He put a thumb and forefinger in the

corners of his mouth and pulled them forward until they joined on his lower lip.

"Did you write it, Clinton?"

The curator reacted as if he had been struck and his eyes darted about among possible lies.

"Webster had kept a diary of our days together, no more. It could not have been twenty pages in all."

"There's no such diary!"

"Is that missing too?"

"Too?" Clinton was caught in his own lie.

"The notebook Webster kept. The diary you based your story on."

"My story? What do you mean?"

"How self-effacing you are, Clinton. But I suppose you have to be. You've created a sensation and now you can't claim credit. Have you been tempted to announce your authorship?"

Vanity undid the lad. He could not keep the smile of pleasure from his thin lips. Had he told no one?

"Or did your wife write it?"

"My wife." He made a sound of contempt.

"Can you trust her?"

"There's nothing to trust!" But it was a feeble attempt to resume his deception. The suggestion that his wife had written the novella drew his contempt and the reverse of that was the pride he took in having done it himself. Clinton was on his feet, turned toward the stove. "More coffee?"

"A brandy would be better. I want to drink a toast to you, Clinton."

Clinton got giddy on authorial pride as much as brandy. What a relief it was for him to admit the novella was his.

"I thought the publisher would suspect, that he would know it wasn't Webster's, but his immediate reaction was such that there was no going back. Later I showed him poems, certain he would know those were mine and the truth about the novella would come out too. What could anyone do to me? The story had been bought and read by hundreds of thousands of readers. I had taken no money. Do you know how much money that little book has earned?"

Clinton knew, to the dime. What an odious man he was, a caricature of the desiccated academic, a type Webster had hated the more because for so long he had lived among them. They were leeches who attached themself to writers and sucked a secondary reputation from them. In the news-magazine story that Webster still carried with him, Clinton was called the leading expert on the poet of whose papers he had become the custodian. But what kind of admirer would foist his own work onto the departed object of his scholarly devotion? The novella was bad enough, but poems! Good God. It angered Webster more that this unprepossessing para-site had dared to affix the name Howard Webster to his own products. Yet what Clinton had done had captivated many, a million readers, in the case of the novella. How much of that interest had spilled back onto authentic Websteriana? That all his books were once more in print was no compensa-tion for what Clinton had done.

"What did you do with Webster's notebook?"

"It's safe."

"But missing?"

"Would you like to see it?"

"Yes."

"I'll get it for you."

Clinton loped into the study and Webster put down his glass. How odd the effect of liquor was. He did not enjoy it as he had, the fuzzy loss of control.

4

OBER'S MALEVOLENT eye seemed to penetrate to Clinton's very soul, and the custodian felt sordid, robbed of the almost hysterical satisfaction he had known since the acceptance, the publication, the critical and commercial success of *The Leaden Echo*. There had been times, as Ober suggested, when he had determined to lay public claim to the achievement, but those were rare moments. For the most part, he had been content to nurse in the recesses of his self the enormous sense of accomplishment the novella had given him. He had not told Jane, he had scarcely formulated the secret to himself, and now this breezy brazen bastard had reappeared from nowhere and somehow instantly guessed what had occurred.

Ober held the balloon glass before him, turning it slowly as if it were a gyroscope, studying Clinton with a little smirk.

"You must have worried that I would return."

"I never thought of it."

The smile broadened but the eyes grew colder. No wonder

Webster had thought of this man as his alter ego. He seemed the dark side of the poet's soul, what poor Webster had thought he was, a failure, forgotten. But Ober was the only one other than Webster himself who could have known of the great literary hoax Clinton had perpetrated.

"Oh, come now. Your conscience can't be clear. Not many men would have the daring to appropriate the reputation of another, to exploit their situation as you have."

Anger flared up in Clinton. He had tried all those arguments on himself and had ended by rejecting them. What he had done was bring to fruition what Webster had begun.

"The novella was Webster's. He had left it worked out as a whole, it had a beginning, a middle and an end."

"There were perhaps twenty pages of notes."

"It was all there!"

Ober waggled his glass, wanting more, but after Clinton poured it, Ober stood and swaggered out of the room. Clinton listened to him slowly climb the steps and heard him overhead. He was in Webster's bedroom. The bastard was using the poet's bathroom. Jane had never trusted the plumbing in the house. When the toilet upstairs flushed the wall of the library seemed to fill with the prolonged sound of rushing water. Webster had left a fragment of a poem which had linked the sound of his flushing toilet to the cloaca maxima seen in the excavation beneath San Clemente in Rome.

Ober came slowly down the stairs and stood in the doorway. "The house is like a shrine. He would have liked that."

"Do you consider yourself an expert on what he would and would not have liked?"

"Don't I have as much right to do that as you? You never met him, did you?"

"Never met him! I began writing on him a dozen years ago."

"How grateful he must have been." Ober sat and picked

up his glass. Before he drank, he said, "If only he had known that you would become his collaborator."

Clinton had thought of publishing the notebook as Webster had left it. But it would not have been a volume, not unless he had surrounded it with the sandwich of his own contribution, an introductory essay placing the manuscript in Webster's oeuvre, notes identifying allusions, correlating Webster's thoughts about Ober with the themes of the poetry. Perhaps photographs of several manuscript pages. But it was while he turned these thoughts over in his mind that the narrative began to take a finished shape in his mind. He started the novella with no conviction that he would do more than see what might become of it if the cryptic notes were expanded. Once he began he could not stop. He thought of the *Kreutzer Sonata* as he wrote, he thought of *The Death of Ivan Ilych*, but he had not taken them as models. The fact is these were Webster's favorites among Tolstoy's works, so thinking of them seemed to ensure that his imagination had become one with the poet's, that he was simply actualizing what lay potentially in the pages of the notebook.

Outside the rain blew up again, washing against the side of the house, the wind howling down the chimney and making the windows rattle.

"A good night to drink," Ober said, but the remark was not convivial. The man's presence was punitive and he clearly meant it to be.

"I don't drink."

"You are drinking."

"It's not a habit of mine."

"You should have acquired it if you intended to become Howard Webster *redivivus*."

"I'll drink beer. I don't like brandy."

"Bring me a beer too."

Clinton would have preferred Ober to keep on downing the brandy. Surely he would get drunk and pass out, at least shut up. What was he supposed to do with this goddam tramp? Webster's reaction to his unwelcome guest was fully understandable now. Why hadn't he just thrown him out? Loneliness. He had wanted someone to talk to, even this stranger, telling him things that shamed him when he noted them in his diary. When Ober asked Clinton to fetch a copy of *The Leaden Echo* he refused at first.

"Clinton, the charade is over, don't you understand? Go get the goddam thing. I've seen it only in Italian."

"Italian!"

But Ober's grin seemed to cancel what he had said. It could have been read in Italian, though—or in Spanish, German, French. The story had been a global success, a publishing phenomenon. That would never have happened if it had been brought out as by Albert Clinton.

"Why do you care about it?"

His right eye half closed. "I don't like to be exploited."

"You prefer exploiting?" Clinton was angry with himself for permitting this interloper to order him about. No doubt this is the way he had moved in on Webster, the legendary camel and the tent, and once in there was no way to dislodge him. It was clear from the diary Webster kept that he and Ober had argued, each of their drinking bouts ending in a shouting match. How had it come to an end?

Ober sat slouched in his chair, holding his glass with both hands as if to warm his beer with body heat. Why did he wear that absurd beret indoors? The lean lines of the vulpine face were emphasized by the beret, seeming to drop like plumb lines from the puffs of frizzy gray hair that sprouted from the cap. The old man's hostility, the belligerence with which he had acted since coming into the house, concentrated Clinton's blurring mind.

"Why have you come back?"

"Why not?"

"Were you still here when . . ."

Ober waited for him to finish the question, but Clinton felt an increased sense of danger. There was no indication in the diary that Ober had left before Webster had performed his final deed, which meant that the tramp might have been still here when Webster lit himself afire. Lit himself afire. Suddenly the simple mechanics of the deed boggled the imagination. Had he crawled atop that huge bonfire and ignited it and then simply sat or lain there until the flames got to him? The ashes in the urn on the mantel were so much after the fact that the sequence of events leading to them could be ignored. Clinton was suddenly struck by the wild incredibility of the standard account of Howard Webster's end.

"I was wakened by the fire," Ober said, tugging at the corners of his mouth as if afraid he would break into a smile.

"You saw him burning?"

"I thought the barn was on fire. If you saw a fire would you imagine that someone was immolating himself? I figured he had gone crazy, that he was lighting fires, that the house might be next. So I left."

He was lying. He was lying in such a way that he appeared to want Clinton to know that he was. Another possibility, what seemed now to be the only plausible explanation, took possession of Clinton's mind. The two men had come to blows, it was what their arguments were destined to become, eventually, a physical fight between two old men. Webster had been injured, perhaps killed. The significance of the funeral pyre became clear. Ober must have thought that burning the body would destroy all the evidence, that without a body there could be no charge. In any case, he had disappeared. And now he was back. Why?

"Imagine my surprise when I learned what had happened. My horror." But he smiled as he said it, negating the sense of his word. Clinton felt like a bee caught by a boy in a jar, some clover thrown in with him, holes punched in the cover. How many boys ever let the bees they caught go free?

"Those are his ashes." Clinton rose and followed his pointing finger to the mantel. This was an effort to induce seriousness in Ober. After all, they were talking about the death of a man, however it had come about.

"His ashes!"

Ober lifted his chin and his manner changed. He put down his glass and lay his palms flat on the arms of his chair. He tipped forward and pushed himself erect, all the while continuing to stare at the urn of ashes. Clinton traced the design in the pottery, angled lines forming a kind of maze.

"How could his ashes . . ."

"Oh, it's a mixture," Clinton said breezily, reoccupying his role as custodian. Thus he had spoken to those who had come to visit the great writer's shrine. He stood facing the room, his body angled slightly toward the urn, his hand now resting on the mantel just short of the Mexican pot. "But even if only one percent should be the ashes of Howard Webster, that is something. It is all we have."

Once or twice he had suggested that the visitation of graves involved regarding with reverent loss as much ground as cadaver, but his listeners had winced at the comparison. He had learned it was best simply to make the point that some at least of the ashes in the pot were the mortal remains of Howard Webster.

"You just keep it there like that, on the mantel?"

"It's convenient."

"Convenient to what, for God's sake?"

Not wanting to lose the advantage he had oddly gained, Clinton took the pot from the mantel, holding it by the neck. Ober's eyes moved with the movement of the pot. He was mesmerized by the ashes.

"Visitors react differently to being told what's in the pot. Some back out of the room. I caught one person trying to take some of the ashes."

"I'm surprised you don't sell samples. In little plastic envelopes. 'Alas, poor Yorick, I knew him well, Horatio.' "

"Webster remarked on your knowledge of Shakespeare."

Ober looked at him, nonplussed.

"In the diary."

Ober reached for the pot, but Clinton moved it out of his reach. "Better not. You've been drinking. We wouldn't want an accident."

"Ha. You could fill it with anything and the tourists wouldn't know the difference."

"But *I* would."

Ober went back to his chair. "Let's have another beer."

"We've had enough beer."

"Well, brandy then."

It seemed a way of ridding himself of the man, not that he felt he had much of a choice. He could imagine Ober picking a fight with him as well, perhaps with consequences similar to his argument with Webster. But he shook the thought away. He must not grant wild speculation the status of fact.

When he returned, he put on a video of Webster reading and Ober watched it with fascination and in silence.

Clinton had no idea how long he could stay awake. Suddenly he was more sleepy that he had been in weeks. He yawned, wanting to ventilate his brain, wanting to ponder the significance of Ober's return and his knowledge or guess about the novella. How could things go on with such a thing known? The accusation alone would disrupt what had become the even tenor of his ways. He thought of life without the job that had come as such a blessing a year and a half before. He felt resentment against Jane, justifiably enough, certainly. If she had accepted the solitude, been willing to make their life here, would he have developed the novella from Webster's notes? He closed his eyes, imagining the reaction if it became known that an obscure custodian had brought off such a literary coup. He was still smiling when he drifted off to sleep.

5

IN THE Bide Awhile Motel in the village, Philip went next door to the unit in which Roger lay like a beached whale on the king-size bed in what was called somewhat pathetically the bridal suite. The thought of any couple beginning their life together in those shabby surroundings did not gladden the heart. Roger's head reposed on a stack of pillows and he looked with rheumy eye at the television whose picture tumbled slowly. Philip adjusted the set and Roger groaned his thanks.

"How do you feel?"

Roger snuffled by way of answer. He pulled tissues from a box on the bed as if they were flower petals. Love me, love me not. But Roger looked unloved and miserable, down with the cold picked up the day before, sloshing around the shrine of Howard Webster. Philip felt guilty for having brought Roger on the trip, but it would have been impossible to leave him in Rye.

"What are you doing?"

Roger had rolled to the edge of the bed and thrown back the covers. "Got to get up."

"You better stay right where you are."

Roger looked around the room with an abject expression. "We didn't drive all this way so I could lie around in a motel."

"I'll see what the drugstore has in the way of cold remedies."

"Anything to stop my nose from running."

In Rye in the bathroom cabinet would be found exactly what Roger wanted, but it was a good question whether any store in the village would be well stocked with such effete preparations. The people here looked as if a broken limb might keep them bedridden but certainly not a cold, if they even got them.

The druggist was also a doctor and he came from his consulting room when the clerk, his wife, gave him a ring. Philip's inquiry had clearly stirred dreams of avarice in the short fat woman with ringlets of rusty hair falling over her forehead. Her husband, tall, stooped, thin, joined them. As a couple these two were out of *Mother Goose*. Philip wondered if they had honeymooned at the Bide Awhile.

"My brother's come down with a very bad cold. We're staying at the motel."

"The Bide Awhile?"

Were there two? "Yes."

He exchanged a glance with his wife. "I'll get my bag."

His wife thrust an umbrella into his hand as he left, although it was not raining at the moment. It seemed a rebuke for Roger's carelessness the day before. When he let them into Roger's unit they were met by the roar of the television. Roger was sitting on the corner of the bed, causing it to tip, and he leaned forward, staring at the screen.

"Philip, look at this."

"I've brought the doctor."

"Listen to this idiotic game."

On the screen contestants were engaged in a game no more idiotic than other television games, but then Roger led a sheltered existence.

"This is Doctor Thorwald, Roger."

Roger had closed his eyes and was breathing rapidly through his nose. He sneezed. Thorwald pulled the door more tightly shut. He put his bag on a desk and opened it.

"Let's take a look at your throat."

"I've got a cold."

Thorwald smiled away this simplistic explanation in the time-honored manner of his profession. He draped a stethoscope around his neck and stood before Roger with a tongue depressor.

Fifteen minutes later, unable to find any more lucrative ailment than the cold, Thorwald scribbled a prescription, was about to hand it to Philip but decided to keep it.

"I'll have my wife bring it over."

"Oh, I'll come get it."

"All I need is a decongestant," Roger said.

Thorwald ignored him. Philip handed the doctor his umbrella and opened the door. It had begun to rain.

Some hours later, Roger was feeling much better, not least because Mrs. Thorwald had brought over a thermos of soup, and the decongestants Philip had managed to buy when the doctor was preparing the prescription, frowning over the instructions he had written to himself, had powerfully assisted the potion Thorwald mixed up. There seemed no reason not to go back to the farm.

The house gleamed whitely in the gloomy day. Water dripped from the trees and the muddy drive when they turned off the road muffled their passage. Despite the already twilit afternoon there were no lights on in the house. There was no car parked by the barn.

"Maybe he stayed in Madison today," Philip said.

Roger snuffled for the first time since they'd left the motel. "I'll try the door."

It seemed best to prove his theory. Roger could not be more disappointed than he was. The prospect of returning to the motel did not please. It would be a good day to sleep, if Roger could be left to himself. The back door was open. Philip tried the handle, sure it would be locked, there seemed no one about the place, but the door pushed open. The sound of the door slamming caused him to turn around. Somehow Roger had gotten out of the van unassisted and was splashing his way to the porch.

"Roger, for the love of God!"

"Amen." He lifted a sandled foot onto the first step and Philip pulled him aboard. "I saw the door open."

They stood for a moment in the kitchen, listening, but there was no sound. Roger shuffled toward the library, calling softly, as if he feared to find the custodian in. "Clinton, Clinton."

Technically this was trespassing, but it could hardly be called malicious. Philip was convinced the curator was not there. Imagine leaving the house unlocked, after having had some documents stolen already. Clinton looked no weirder than others of his kind, but Philip would not have suspected such carelessness. On the contrary. Clinton was the fussy sort. It was that which had made the missing manuscript so difficult to understand. Had Clinton ever lost anything in his life?

Roger went on into the study but Philip sat down in the library. A nice collection of books, aesthetically; they were arrayed upon their shelves, soft reds and browns, beautifully bound books but most with their gaudy dust jackets still on. Taken simply as decor, there is nothing to equal books. It was not a sentiment shared by Roger. He preferred paperbacks to hardcovers, thought collecting books as possessions anachronistic.

"Before the invention of movable type, the single copy of a book was a treasure, even apart from illumination and gilt. Incunabula were precious in their day, not just subsequently. But in the contemporary world, with mass-market paperbacks even of learned works, with photocopying and above all the computer, individual copies of information are as objects worthless. One might just as well collect old automobiles."

"People do."

"I know. And drive them only with trepidation."

Roger's collection belied this sentiment. Had he ever thrown away a book? He treated them as if they were fragile or precious. His spidery writing filled the margins and flyleafs of most of his books. Reading for him was largely a matter of entering into an argument with the author.

"Philip, come here."

"What is it?"

"I think you have accomplished your mission."

Roger sat at Webster's desk in the study. With a letter opener he had been turning over pages from the small pile on the desk.

"What's that?"

"The missing manuscript."

"You're sure?"

"Oh yes. This is the text but more important this is Webster's hand."

"So Clinton found it."

"If it was lost."

Using the letter opener, Roger flipped the pages back into a neat pile. He seemed to be exercising an almost clinical care. He sat there looking at the pile of pages, his nose a wrinkled walnut as he frowned. If he thought Clinton had known where the manuscript was and produced it after they left the previous day this did not please him.

"That has to be it, Roger. His car isn't here, he must be in Madison."

"You think he got it out from a hiding place, put it here

where we would find it and thoughtfully left the house unlocked."

"It sounds plausible to me."

"Then call Madison and see if he's there."

Why are there certain simple tasks we do not wish to undertake? "You do it."

"It's your idea."

He had to stop himself from continuing the childish exchange. "You get his number and I'll call him."

As luck would have it, the Madison number was on a slip of paper in the desk, as if Clinton himself was afraid he'd forget it. Philip dialed the number.

"Yes?" A woman's voice.

"Mr. Clinton, please."

"Could I take a message? He isn't here just now."

"When do you expect him back?"

"Who is this?"

"Philip Knight. Mrs. Leamon asked me to look into the missing manuscript. I talked to your husband yesterday . . ."

"He's at the Webster farm. He stayed there overnight."

Philip made a face at Roger. "Thank you very much, Mrs. Clinton."

"When you see him, tell him to call home, will you?"

Roger acted as if it was his own theory that had been disproved. "His car is gone?"

"Yes."

"He's not in the house. Where would he be?"

The kitchen looked spick-and-span. In the garbage were a surprising number of dead soldiers. Clinton had drunk a twelve-pack since he last took out the garbage. That seemed pretty heavy drinking for a curator. Roger came into the kitchen and lumbered to the back door where he stared out at the rain. He pushed the screen door open and stepped onto the porch. Philip went back to the study for a closer look at the manuscript of *The Leaden Echo*. Inspired by

Roger's caution, he did not touch the pages, sliding the top one off, then the next. He had not read the novella, settling for Roger's reading it to him. A gripping story, no doubt about that. Poor Clinton. No doubt the curator had planned to unload the manuscript on the black market. A risky thing to do even if his motive was to get money enough to change jobs. However much Clinton liked this solitary job, it was pretty clear his wife did not. Not many husbands continue in jobs strongly vetoed by their wives.

The sound of Roger's hollering came to him, and he pushed back from the desk. He hurried through the house and out onto the back porch, prepared for anything, very likely Roger lying in a mud puddle. But his brother was standing in front of the open barn doors. He gestured Philip to come.

Picking his way across the yard, Philip remembered the novel. Odd how that story seemed to be part of the real history of this farm. Roger stepped aside and Philip looked into the gloom of the barn. His first impression was of dryness and quiet. And then he saw the body.

Clinton hung from a beam that formed the outer edge of the hayloft.

"Dear God," Roger said in a husky whisper.

Philip went into the barn to cut down the body. Not that it mattered. Clinton was no longer of this world. Like the poet he admired, he had gone to that bourn from which no traveler returns.

BOOK TWO

1
PART ONE

"BETTER NOT, Philip," Roger said as Philip neared the hanging body. "Shouldn't he be found as we found him?"

"I just wanted to make sure he's dead."

Roger stood where he had been standing when Philip came out of the house, his great body seeming to take root in the muddy earth. The rain soaked his hair and ran down the chubby geography of his face. However pained his brother's expression, Philip knew that there was nothing of this scene that Roger would not be able to recall. If he lived, that is. Standing out in the rain with the cold he had was suicidal.

"Let's go inside, Roger."

Like a kid, Roger avoided no puddle he could splash through. His body swayed as they walked and he began to moan.

"Think of his poor wife, Phil."

"The police can give her the bad news."

Roger's reaction, though silent, told Philip what he thought of that suggestion.

When they got to the porch, out of the rain, Roger stopped again and they listened to the steady sound of the rain, a sibilant language they could not quite understand.

"How long has he been out there, Philip?"

"Why don't we let the police find the answer to questions like that?"

The police in this case amounted to a man named Bunting who stood with his hat low on his eyes and the hands in his coat pockets wrapping that garment around him like a furled flag while water dripped from the soaked cuffs of his trousers. Beside him, bright and ready for duty, was Dr. Thorwald in his capacity of deputy county coroner.

"Why'd ya look in the barn?" Bunting asked.

"Have you read the novella *The Leaden Echo*?" Roger asked him.

Bunting made a slow turn and looked at Thorwald, then turned back to Roger. "That book out in the barn?"

Mrs. Thorwald had been in the kitchen, pouring coffee from the large thermoses she had brought, looking about birdlike over her tray of Styrofoam cups. Roger got served first, perhaps out of deference to his ailment, and when all were provided with coffee, Philip took over. Roger understood only imperfectly the ordinary man's desire for ordinary facts. Bunting tipped back the brim of his hat as Philip spoke and the water that began to drip steadily from it might have been measuring the time Philip was accorded to explain their discovery of Clinton's dead body in the barn.

"Why'd he go all the way out to the barn to kill himself?" Bunting wanted to know.

"It was raining last night too." Mrs. Thorwald shook her head and cocked her head at Roger, keeping her eye on the floor at her feet as if on the alert for the squirm of a worm.

"Body wet, Glen?"

"The clothes were damp. Not soaked."

"You think maybe he ran out there?" The wide mouth

of Bunting dimpled at its corners, then spread into a large lugubrious smile. "Hurry up and die?"

"Okay if I take the body away now, Ned?" asked Dr. Thorwald.

Bunting adjusted the brim of his hat, stopping the rain that had been dripping down his back, and looked around. Everybody but Roger still stood, taking their cue from Bunting who was making an effort to remember what he was supposed to do in such a set of circumstances.

"What'd we do with Jake last October?"

"Took a lot of pictures, then I took the body away."

"His wife ran him down with the tractor," Mrs. Thorwald said to Roger in a stage whisper. "His dog reported her."

"What?"

But that side conversation was drowned out by Bunting explaining to Thorwald that he couldn't take pictures in the dark and the deputy coroner, pharmacist, general practitioner, countering with a tale of the marvels of the flash bulb. Philip had not begun with any confidence in these two, but what little there was went now. Not that he particularly lamented this. Clinton's suicide seemed to present no mystery.

"No mystery!" Roger said, wheezing and snuffling in the van when finally they headed back to the Bide Awhile. "What about the manuscript?"

"But it's back."

"Of course it's back. Why?"

So Philip told Roger what he assumed anyone would think. Clinton had considered stealing the holograph, for some reason thought better of it, though Philip was inclined to think that the lengthy exchange between Clinton and Roger played some role in that. Had Clinton realized that an aficionado like Roger would never accept the loss of the manuscript? Felicia Leamon's determination to locate it might diminish and go, Philip would give it his best shot and still not find it, but Roger would go to the ends of the earth—metaphorically, that is, this visit to Wisconsin was one of his few voluntary excursions out of Rye—and expend every bit of his brother's energy until the handwritten version of *The Leaden Echo* was found. Intuitively aware of this, Clinton had put the manuscript on the desk and, in despair at his intended perfidy, gone away and hanged himself.

"Like Judas?"

"I would never have thought of the analogy."

"Your account misses few opportunities for bogus drama."

"Bogus?"

"You say he committed suicide. How?"

"Roger, the logistics of self-slaughter are notoriously bizarre. How did he string himself that high? I don't know. You saw the sawhorse."

"But he didn't die by hanging."

Twenty yards ahead, a deer appeared in the headlights, a beautiful silhouette of a leaping doe, there for a chiaroscuro moment, then gone.

"I see. He is dead, though, isn't he?"

"God rest his soul."

"We did find him hanging by the neck in the barn, stone-cold dead, did we not?"

"Yes, yes."

"One would tend to add those facts together and say he hanged himself."

"Of course. We were meant to, I suppose."

"By whom?"

"By the one who drove away in Clinton's car."

"Did you see that deer?"

"She was beautiful."

Roger had once quoted a description of some ideal kind of human, a man on whom nothing was lost, something like that. To Philip such sensibility seemed a curse rather than a blessing, imagine going through a large city and noticing, actually noticing, everything going on around you. But blessing or curse, his brother Roger had it.

"What did Mrs. Thorwald mean when she said the farmer's dog turned in the wife?"

"Ben, that was the dog's name, picked up the severed arm of his master and ran to town and dropped it at Bunting's feet."

"You believe that?"

"Mrs. Thorwald does."

"That doesn't answer my question."

"I suppose it's a case of reverse retrieval. But it was something he was trained to do. Jake trained Ben to take his lunch bucket to the house for a refill when he was working in the field. The hand of the arm Ben brought to town clutched the canteen from which Jake had been drinking when she shot him with a twenty-two and then proceeded to drive over him with the tractor, apparently to make it look like an accident. The reaper was attached, that severed the arm, Ben picked up the canteen and the arm as well and ran to town."

"Why Bunting?"

"He runs a saloon on the side."

"No wonder you want to dream up a fanciful explanation for what happened to Clinton."

"Where do you think the car went?"

All the rest might seem as farfetched as Mrs. Thorwald's account of how Jake's wife had been found guilty of murder, but the missing car was a plain unvarnished fact, no doubt of that. When they arrived at the farm earlier, they had assumed Clinton was still in Madison, which is where he had said he was going when they last saw him. He went to Madison every afternoon and came back in the morning, Monday through Friday, the neighbors along the road would attest to that. He had not gone. His wife had not seen him. No wonder about that, he hung dead in the barn. But his car was gone.

2

ON THE drive to the village, Felicia put the car on cruise control and sat pensively at the wheel, being borne westward to a place she had learned to hate while her father was alive. The man who had made life such a hell for her mother, who had lived a completely self-indulgent life, who had married Aran despite or perhaps because she was Felicia's friend, who sat out there in solitude, continuing to write as if all were well with the world, had become her definition of injustice. A man like that should suffer as he had made others suffer. Instead, he was celebrated, anthologized, spoken of with awe, as Aran had spoken of him once. The best revenge Felicia could devise was the Webster Foundation. Let his name continue to be celebrated, she would not take a nickel from any estate he might have. And at the time of his death, there had been little.

When the foundation was set up, the assets were the farm, the papers, the thin trickle of royalties. What an ironic comment on her father's promethean dreams of success as a poet.

The foundation and the farm as shrine had been a condemnation of her dead hated father. Clinton had seemed the perfect ineffectual academic to move in there with his whiny wife and by their very presence comment on the meagerness of Howard Webster's achievement.

What had happened in the past year and a half had turned the tables on her revenge. The father she had thought to embalm in his fallen inconsequential reputation proved to have saved his best work for posthumous publication. When Clinton first mentioned the novella to her and his hope to have it published, Felicia had felt no intuitive tremor at what lay ahead. Suddenly there was money in abundance and the name of Howard Webster shone in the firmament as it never had before. And Felicia was left to realize that what she should have done was sell the farm, box up the papers and books and put them in storage.

Nor would she have had recourse to such an ass as Cannon to set up the foundation. Oh, that had been one thing, the legal work that any lawyer could have done; the truly stupid thing was to accept his suggestion that he become an officer of the foundation and bring in his obsequious assistant Baum. At the time, it had all seemed a legal fiction anyway, a device to hang on to the farm at least for a while, until the lump sum from her father's retirement program at the University of Wisconsin was exhausted. Clinton seemed the perfect complement to Cannon. And then that turkey-necked academic discovered *The Leaden Echo* and the world-wide literary sensation brought money pouring into the coffers of the Webster Foundation, turning the hitherto comic Cannon into an annoying competitor.

Almost as bad a revelation was Frank's financial condition. She had always assumed that, since he was so successful a man, their financial situation was secure.

"Letters from my father? Why?"

"Don't you realize how valuable they could be now?"

"There are cabinets full of letters at the farm. He was a man of letters." A self-description in a long piece in *The Atlantic*, Howard Webster describing himself as a member of the last generation of writers who wrote letters. No longer would a literary man be honored by the collection of his correspondence. Look at the letters of James, of Stevenson, of Howells. Even Van Gogh, with his letters to Theo. Writers now would be remembered for their telegrams, at most, and, of late, Fax messages. In the files of literary agents would be found the curt exchanges on contracts and offers, but what else would there be except the published work? And even in the case of the published work, there would be no drafts, no evolving stages of the manuscript, at most the computer disk on which the final version went to an editor. By contrast, her father wrote, in the case of his own generation, the published work would be but the tip of an iceberg, the apex of a mountain of paper. It was an article Clinton had drawn on in his first descriptive bulletin on the Webster Foundation and it seemed to foretell the discovery of the hitherto undreamt-of novella.

"You must have saved some of his letters."

"Frank, you know what I thought of my father. Why would I have kept anything of his, presuming he'd written me?"

"How about your mother?"

In the attic, in a small dented metal trunk her parents had used on their first trip to Europe, were packets of letters. Letters from her mother to her father, written on lined stationery paper, an unformed hand, with misspellings, the regular placement of *e* before *i* except after *c* as if she had simply gotten the rule wrong, the letters written at night after clerking in a store in Davenport—"There was a clerk of Davenport," was some doggerel this prompted from her father, who was doing graduate work in English at the University of Minnesota but actually, as later became part of the legend, sitting most days all day in Stub and Herb's in a back booth, reading and writing and talking and wooing anything in a skirt. And writing seemingly sincere letters of love to her mother in Davenport. "There's nothing half worth havin', as my little port in Daven," etc.—it was difficult to see in those jocular bits of verse scattered through his letters the promise of the poet he became. There was also her mother's diary kept during the first European trip, with its entry computing Felicia's conception in Florence in May when they were both full of wine and the thrill of Italy.

Felicia sat in the hot attic, eyes filled with tears, looking through the dusty air at the linen curtain covering the round dormer window, filled with sunlight. How vulnerable her mother seemed, relying on the faithful love of Howard Webster, bearing his child, exultant at the fact. And Felicia thought of her own vulnerability, that scarcely begun life, with so many months in which something could go wrong. God knows, her father had made no concessions to his wife's pregnancy. The grand tour continued through the following year, he got an extension of his Fulbright grant, and her mother went home to Davenport where Felicia was born. She traced with the tip of her finger the lines her mother had written so long ago and again felt dizzy at the difference between what her mother could know of her future when she wrote and what Felicia knew now as she read. Is life tolerable only because of how little we know of the context of our doings?

"I have letters of mother's."

Frank pressed the tip of his nose, wondering. "Maybe they would be worth something. Where did you find them?"

"I never lost them," she lied. She had not felt strong enough to look in her mother's trunk before Frank's mention of letters.

"Who are they written to?"

"My father."

"Then he must have written to her."

She gave him, as the least valuable thing of her mother's and the most valuable as it pertained to her father's life, the notebook in which her mother had recorded their first European travels, the hotels, the amounts spent on food and lodgings, little lists of what they had seen. The mention of getting pregnant in Florence. Frank might have been more pleased when she presented it to him.

"How will you go about selling it?"

"If I can."

The obvious worry with which he spoke drove away her annoyance at his ingratitude. "How bad are things?"

"Oh, it's just temporary."

"Tell me."

He took her in his arms. "Sweetheart, I don't want to trouble you with the ups and downs of business."

In the end it was Mrs. Metzger, his secretary, who told her how things were.

"Have I ever told you anything about your husband's business dealings, Felicia?"

"Mrs. Metzger, he's obviously in a bad way. I want to know how bad."

Mrs. Metzger put her hand on Felicia's, then removed it so the waitress could lay out their tea. They sat in the roof garden of the Marlin Hotel, surrounded by cosseted corseted pampered consorts of the well-to-do of Milwaukee.

"I only said that as preface to the fact that I intend to break a confidence now. Has Frank ever mentioned Hector?"

Felicia laughed. "The wheeler-dealer? I know Frank gets a kick out of his wild schemes."

"So he's told you about them?"

Obviously Mrs. Metzger had something more in mind than the antics of an entrepreneurial clown. "Tell me."

She went on drinking tea, she ate her buttered toast with a little marmalade, she nodded to keep Mrs. Metzger talking, but it was like listening to things that involved a stranger, not a series of financial failures that affected her as well.

When Clinton called to tell her that the manuscript of *The Leaden Echo* was missing, Felicia's first thought was that Frank had taken it. She went up to the attic and opened the green metal trunk and was not surprised to find the bundle of her father's letters missing.

Now driving to the village, having left a message for Frank on the phone at home, she stared at the wet road and fought the conviction that her husband had something to do with the death of the curator.

3

IN THE privacy of his office, Frank took the change from his pocket and checked the dates on the coins. The silver was of recent date, but the pennies looked promising. He separated out the three or four that were blackened with age, put the rest of the change in his pocket, and tilted the pennies to the light. 1954! He didn't trust his eyes at first, and shifted the coin so that the light fell more surely on it. It was true, the date was that of his birth. He would not have described himself as a superstitious man. If anything, he thought of himself as a child of his times, marked by the scientific method. He favored a rational approach, hence the elaborate business plans with which he had impressed Hector and others. But such computerized marvels merely masked his willingness to go against any and every fact so long as his instincts pressed him on. No wonder he consulted the numbers on paper money for winning poker hands. No wonder he consulted the dates on coins for corroboration of his hunch that his life was about to take a turn for the better.

To have found a penny minted in the year of his birth was like feeling the hand of God on his shoulder. But the other date was more significant still. 1977. The year of his first marriage. The most cogent interpretation of these two lucky coins was that he would finally enjoy the business success he longed for.

The travel diary had brought six thousand, a price Frank would not settle for today, knowing more about the traffic in literary memorabilia than he had on his California visit. Now Hector suggested that he deal with a man in Princeton, a man of reputation.

"I can't be running off to New Jersey."

"I'll go but of course I'll need authorization," Hector had said. "Hollander won't even look at anything if I can't supply proof of ownership or assignment of the power to negotiate purchase."

The fact that he owed Hector money seemed to make him the ideal deputy. He was not likely to settle for too little.

"I wish you had that missing manuscript too, Frank."

"It's no longer missing."

"No kidding."

"The curator's dead. Apparently a suicide. Felicia is out there now."

Leaving the coast clear so Frank could take her father's letters. Well, if he could meet his bills, and get back onto the business plan, there would be more than enough money to make up for the loss of the letters. He had the look of a man who had just done something he could not undo and was beginning to feel regret.

"I'm lucky she hadn't burned them. She hated her father."

"You keep saying that."

"Do I? It's true."

"Some hatred, starting the foundation, pumping all the money back into that effort to keep her father's name alive."

"That wasn't her intention."

Now he waited while Hector was off to Princeton. If he himself had gone, he would have taken Amtrak. It took too much time, but it was better than sweating bullets on a plane. He hated flying and flew only reluctantly. Flights were too fast and made him too uneasy to think, but trains were something else. Just sitting there, unable to do anything else even if he wanted to, Frank knew the only contemplative moments in his life. As the train rocked along he filled his head with schemes and it was amazing how the ideas came as he rode. Much as he could now, mooning here over dreams of avarice and what the successful outcome of Hector's mission could mean. It had been like sending a child to the store, securing the packet of letters in the inside pocket of Hector's jacket.

Too bad about the curator but the fact that a major manuscript was not on the market would boost the value of the letters. Supply and demand. He remembered Hector saying, You give me a Webster manuscript, now, and we can really do business. Well, there weren't any Howard Webster manuscripts on the market and as for the travel record, the purchaser had lied about what he paid for it, tripling the sum, probably what Frank could have gotten, but that was okay too, it set a standard Hollander would have to meet.

He told himself he did not feel bad because he was about to sell Howard Webster's letters without Felicia's permission. She hated her father. She never tired of telling him that. Frank was not sure he believed her. No matter how you sliced it there was the foundation and the appearance at least of a daughter devoted to the memory of her father. Frank tried to talk himself into believing it so that taking mementos of her father did not bother his conscience so much. He did not understand Felicia. Just as he had not understood Marge.

"Why did you leave me?" he'd asked her in California. "What made you hate me?"

"Frank, I don't hate you. I still like you. But we were

meant for only a couple years and we had it. Besides, you're
the one who married again, not me. Let's just be friends."

Friends! He wished now that Marge did hate him, hate
him the way Felicia hated her father.

What it came down to was you can only hate those you
love and the fact that Marge was so goddam casual about
smashing a marriage told him it had never meant much to
her. We were meant for a couple years! Is that what she'd
told herself at the beginning? Had she stood there when they
got married thinking I'll take Frank Leamon for a few years,
until it gets boring, until I decide to go to California or
whatever? He couldn't believe that, not that she had thought
it out clearly, but it must have there at the time somehow,
beneath the surface.

Throughout the night, bouncing around sleepless in his
bed, he imagined Hector making ten thou apiece on the
letters. If he came home rolling in dough, as his father used
to say, there was no way in the world Felicia wouldn't forgive
him for selling what belonged to her.

4

THE ROOM had a ten foot ceiling, pale green walls but above the picture rail chalk white began. A sink in one corner, a wardrobe, hardwood floors, a radiator from which pipes rose to the ceiling and sank into the floor. Where did convents get beds so narrow as this one? Perhaps they were tailor made for those who took the vow of chastity. The easy chair, so to speak, had wooden arms and green plastic cushions, and there was a straight chair at the lemon-colored laminated desk on top of which an el cheapo lamp stood, the only other light in the room being a milky globe enclosed ceiling lamp. A smoke detector looked down on Felicia too as she lay on the bed, her arms at her side, conscious of how hateful this room was, yet loving it.

The convent in central Wisconsin was the retirement home of the order that taught in the college Felicia had attended. She and Frank had been generous contributors and her reward was to be an honored guest at Presentation Convent whenever she spent more than a day at the farm.

The convent was twelve miles to the west of the farm, close enough, far enough. That afternoon she had stopped in the village and talked to Dr. Thorwald about Clinton.

"Has his wife been notified?"

"I didn't know he had a wife. I don't think Bunting knows either."

"Then she hasn't been told?"

He rolled out his lower lip, the corners of his mouth dropped, his shoulders rose and fell.

"I'll call her," she said, unnecessarily.

That unwelcome duty decided her to go right on to the convent where Sister Rose Alma, using two canes, made her painful progress to the front door, her large-toothed smile seeming to deny that it was a nuisance for her to walk. But she was the porter and answering the door was her path to heaven so she dragged herself along with a sunny smile.

"Felicia, what good time you made." Sister Rose Alma swung back from the door, to let Felicia in.

"I stopped in the village."

The nun went into a spasm of incredulity. When was the last time she had made the trip to or from Milwaukee?

"Such a car you must have."

The trouble with nuns, they made her want to apologize for everything, for living well in Milwaukee, for not loving her father, for not suspecting the financial trouble Frank was in. A day or two at Presentation and Felicia was painfully aware of all her faults and would drive off resolved to be good as gold in the future, but by the time she went through the village she had shed these edifying thoughts and was eager to get back to the routine she had been disparaging in the privacy of her own mind.

After washing up, she went down the hall to a waiting room where there was a phone. When she closed the door of the room, she felt she was about to broadcast rather than telephone. Before dialing, she said a prayer that Jane would

not be home, that someone had already told her, that . . .
But as is the way with such prayers, hers was unanswered.

"Jane, this is Felicia Leamon."

"Is Clinton with you?"

That ambiguous question told her Jane did not know of
her husband's death and that she was worried about him.

"Jane, something terrible has happened."

Silence. Then, "To Clinton?"

"Yes."

"Tell me!"

Belatedly it occurred to Felicia that she should have gone
to Madison to tell Jane face-to-face. This was not the kind
of news to hear over the telephone. The army, the airlines,
always pay personal visits to the relatives of casualties.

"Jane, I can come to Madison."

"Tell me what's happened to my husband."

Jane's voice rose and in it was the implication that whatever bad news she was about to hear was Felicia's fault.
Perhaps in a way that was true. She had thought of the
foundation out of vindictiveness, she had chosen Clinton
because of his implausibility, he might still be teaching in
Trout Lake if it weren't for Felicia.

"He's dead, isn't he?"

"Yes."

"Oh, my God."

"Jane, can you come up here?"

"How? I haven't a car. Clinton has the car."

As if that were her grievance she began to weep. Holding
the phone pressed to her ear, hearing that inconsolable sobbing as if it came from her own breast, yet also able to
appraise it almost clinically, Felicia told herself it was best
this way.

"Jane, listen to me. Call a cab and come here at once."

"A cab, from Madison?"

"Tell them when you call you want to be taken here. I
will pay the fare. Take down this address."

And she dictated the address of the convent to the suddenly docile Jane. This was no time for the woman to be alone. Besides, there were practical matters to be taken care of with respect to her husband's remains. Felicia could help but more important the nuns could.

After she hung up, Felicia talked to Sister Rose Alma who was delighted by the prospect of more demands on her time and energy. Then Felicia telephoned the Bide Awhile Motel and asked for Philip Knight. The phone rang and rang. Felicia hung up, called the motel again and asked for Roger Knight's unit. The phone was answered on the first ring.

"Philip Knight?"

"Just a moment."

The voice she had heard was that of the brother about whom Philip had spoken in such reverent tones.

"When can I see you?" she asked when Philip came on the line.

"Are you coming out?"

"I'm already here. Nearby. I can be there in fifteen minutes."

This was fine with Philip Knight. Exactly twelve minutes later Felicia pulled in at the Bide Awhile.

"What is the latest news on Clinton?"

His eyes drifted away. "The coroner says it was suicide."

"Dear God. I telephoned his wife. She should be on her way now."

"She's coming from Madison?"

"That's right."

"Driving?" He leaned toward her, his eyes bright. What an odd man.

"I told her to take a cab. She cannot drive because her husband has their car."

He sat back, his eyes no longer bright.

"Is something wrong?"

"No."

At that moment someone began to pound on the door of

the unit and Philip hurried to answer it. He opened the door wide to reveal a man wider than the doorway, an enormously fat man with an oddly youthful face, who looked in at her and then came sideways into the room, more or less squeezing himself in.

"Mrs. Leamon, this is my brother Roger."

Was he retarded? His great flapping trousers were secured by suspenders that were crossed over his chest. On his feet were worn slippers that slapped as he crossed to her. Felicia glanced toward Philip for help in interpreting this advance, but he was beaming as if his brother were performing a daring feat. The fat brother took her hand and brought it to his lips. Felicia was at once charmed and piqued: an honor had been done her but by an imbecile.

"Philip has told me all about you. I am a devotee of Howard Webster's poetry and, though a mere amateur, cede to no one in my admiration for his work."

Felicia nodded, taken aback as much by the remark as by her surprise at hearing this creature say something intelligible. Having spoken, Roger extracted a large bandanna-style handkerchief and blew his nose decisively.

"Roger has caught a terrible cold," Philip said indulgently. "He traipsed around in the mud and rain at the farm yesterday and then again today. It was Roger who discovered the body."

She asked for details and was pleased with the way in which Philip summarized events, at once vivid and concise. She could imagine Roger seated at her father's desk, turning over pages of the reappeared manuscript.

"Clinton put it there?"

Philip nodded. "That appears to be what happened."

"Tell me, Mrs. Leamon," Roger Knight said. "Had you ever seen your father's manuscript of *The Leaden Echo*?"

"No."

"There was a notebook, a running account of a visit from

a man named Ober, and the manuscript. Does the name Ober mean anything to you?"

"He is a character in my father's story, isn't he?"

"You're not sure?"

"Mr. Knight," she said, addressing Roger, "at the risk of shocking you, let me tell you that I am not one of my father's devotees and I know little of his work. The way he treated my mother and me was not conducive to hero worship."

"Your mother was Vivian Bonner?"

"That's right."

"From Davenport, Iowa?"

"So you really are a devotee?"

"Ober is indeed a character in your father's novella. The question is, was he anything more?"

"More?"

"Was he real as well?"

"I haven't any idea."

"Nor have I. But perhaps it does not matter."

Philip Knight said, "My brother doesn't think Clinton's death was a suicide."

"Didn't you say the coroner ruled it a suicide?"

"That's right."

Roger Knight said, "There's reason to think that Clinton was dead before he was strung up in the barn."

"Good Lord, why do you say that?"

"Have you ever seen a hanging?"

"No! Have you?"

"Being hanged tends to break the neck, with death due to strangulation. This produces rather distinctive effects on the features, the tongue . . ."

"That's enough, Roger. What he means is that the effects we associate with hanging were not present in the case of Clinton."

"Are you suggesting that someone hung a dead man up in the barn?"

Philip Knight said, "I felt a duty to mention these suspicions to you. The question is are you satisfied that what you hired me to do no longer needs doing? The missing manuscript is where it belongs. As for Roger's theory, the local authorities would be ill-disposed to listen to it. The deputy coroner has ruled suicide, Ned Bunting doubtless wants to get the whole thing behind him. A year and a half ago there was the dramatic event of your father's death, now there is another suicide at the farm. Bunting is not likely to welcome the suggestion that it wasn't a suicide and I suspect professional vanity will cause Thorwald to stay with his verdict. To overturn it would entail bringing in the county coroner himself."

Felicia had been shaking her head through half of this. "No. You've done what I wanted done."

"Madam, I have done nothing. We have only Clinton's word that a manuscript was missing and now it is not missing. I cannot take credit for something that would have taken place if I had stayed in New York."

"I insist that you send me your bill."

"Only for expenses."

Roger broke in, "If I could have some memento of your father's?"

"I no longer have control over his property. All that is invested in the foundation."

"It was wise of you to set up the foundation," Roger Knight said.

"Far wiser than I knew at the time."

"Do all the proceeds from your father's works go to the foundation?"

"Yes."

"Then you are generous as well as wise."

His praise was salt in the wound.

"There is one consolation," Roger Knight said as she prepared to leave. They were agreed that Philip Knight's mission was accomplished and he could return to Rye. She would cover his expenses and pay a token five-thousand-dollar fee.

"And what is that?"

"You will have no difficulty finding a successor for Clinton. There must be dozens of Webster experts who would kill for such a post."

Since she could not unilaterally dissolve the foundation, it must go on. Roger Knight was correct. A successor to Clinton would have to be appointed, and that at least was hers to do. Well, things had changed since she hired Clinton. Not only was the foundation now richly endowed, it turned out that Frank was hurting badly for money. The conjunction of these two told Felicia what she would be looking for in the new curator. She wanted someone who would cooperate with her to bypass Cannon. She wanted, in short, a patsy because one way or the other she intended to profit from the unexpected and dramatic rise in her father's reputation.

5

THE FOLLOWING day the sun shone and by noon had drawn to itself most of the surface water remaining from the days of rain. Roger, full of medicine and Mrs. Thorwald's chicken soup, looked like several new men and Philip was less eager to put this whole episode behind him. It was seldom that a failed assignment had proved to be so interesting, at least to Roger, and now with the sun out and the Wisconsin countryside resplendently green, Philip found cogency in Roger's suggestion that the nice thing to do would be to stay around and ease Clinton's widow's burden. It was clear that Roger wished to speak with the woman.

His interest was certainly not in clarifying the mysteries that surrounded Philip's assignment, narrowly construed. Roger was moved by his fascination with the writings of Howard Webster. He was intrigued by that farmhouse filled with memorabilia of the great poet, the manuscripts, the prizes, the ambience. Roger had read aloud one of the "Baraboo Elegies" and Philip supposed it was good stuff,

though he certainly was no judge. If Roger had come to
Wisconsin as an appendage to Philip's work, they stayed on
now because of Roger and it was Philip who slipped into the
secondary role. He drove Roger to the convent where Clinton's widow was staying and she came into the parlor and
stood staring back and forth between the two brothers.

"Who are you?"

Roger rose and waddled to her, murmuring something
scarcely coherent about her husband, terrible loss, wonderful
fellow, spoke to him the night before it happened.

"You were at the farm?"

"Roger found your husband's . . ."

Flat thin hair fell indecisively almost to her bony shoulders
and for a woman she had something suspiciously like an
Adam's apple. It would have seemed miraculous that such a
woman had found a husband if she hadn't met Clinton. Her
eyes bulged in horror and Philip stopped.

"How long did the two of you live at the farm?" Roger
asked gently.

"Too long! How I came to hate that place."

"Tell me about it."

For fifteen minutes she told her tale of woe, how alone
she felt at the farm, Clinton had his work, but what was she
supposed to do at the back of beyond with the nearest neighbor half a mile away and wild dogs prowling the countryside?

"Wild dogs?"

Once it appeared she had been frightened by a neighbor's
pet while she was wandering in the woods north of the
house. Her efforts to make it sound terrifying succeeded only
in drawing attention to her exaggerated reaction. That
Clinton had then bought her a dog was put forward as the
QED against remaining on the farm. So they had moved to
Madison.

"Clinton commuted back and forth?"

"Which meant I was left without a car."

She seemed determined to carry on a dozen quarrels with
her husband despite his death.

"Where is his car now?"

"Isn't it at the farm?"

Roger left that question alone and got her talking about
their first weeks at the farm, when she too had thought it an
ideal situation, living quarters rent free, a higher salary than
Clinton had received as a teacher, an area where the cost of
living was as low as anywhere in the Midwest. The prospect
of actually saving money loomed for the first time in their
marriage.

"Did you help him at all with the papers?"

Often in their early idyllic days she had sat in the study
while Clinton worked. As she spoke of this her tone softened
and there crept into her eyes the disturbing doubt that perhaps it was she who had been at fault. But before that
moment arrived, she satisfied Roger's curiosity about how
her husband had worked. She fell silent for a moment, biting
the knuckle of her index finger.

"He should have come home," she said, as if rebutting
an unspoken suggestion. "If he had come home to Madison,
it wouldn't have happened."

If things were different they would be different. Philip
wished this new widow would at least weep for her departed
husband, grieve if only out of a sense of propriety, but she
contained whatever sadness she felt, perhaps because it
seemed directed only at herself.

"Let's stop by the farm," Roger suggested from the back
of the van, spinning in his chair as if he were manning a
gun turret. They were on their way back to the Bide Awhile.

"I had hoped we'd seen the end of the place."

Roger hummed, ignoring the suggestion that some things
in life might be more interesting than the farm of Howard
Webster. Philip fished out the key to the door he'd been
given by Ned Bunting. As the employee of Felicia, Philip

was considered to have more right to the key than anyone else.

"I'd use it if I were you," Bunting said. He meant lock the door.

The house had been empty the day before when they entered but it seemed emptier now, since they had no expectation that anyone would be there. In the study, Roger flicked on the computer and ran a menu on the hard disk.

"Clinton did a good job, Philip. He was well into cataloguing the holdings of the foundation, using a simple but informative description."

"How far had he gotten?"

"He was working backward, cataloguing the latest first. See."

Roger typed *The Leaden Echo* and entered and in a moment the screen filled with information as to where the manuscript could be found. The filing cabinet was the one immediately next to the computer. Roger pulled open the drawer.

"I suppose I should return this manuscript."

He rifled around in the drawer, frowning, then ran the menu again, typed *The Leaden Echo* and entered.

"That's funny. There's no entry for the manuscript, only the notebook."

"Nothing funny about that. He must have erased all reference to the manuscript when he decided to steal it."

"It should have left a bigger gap in the drawer then."

Clinton must have feared he was going to run out of filing cabinets. The drawer Roger had opened was tightly packed with manila envelopes, each containing papers separated by acid-free archival sheets in order to increase their longevity.

"Maybe he moved things up from the next drawer."

"Maybe. I'll make room for this and put it away."

But he began to turn over the pages again and became absorbed in the story. Philip went upstairs, to take a final tour of the house. When they left and locked it up it might be empty for some time. Unless Felicia hired a new curator immediately. The bedrooms had not been used for months, probably since Jane had persuaded her husband to move to Madison. These spaces had once contained the living Webster, his wife and friends, but they were less suggestive of life than the manuscripts downstairs. The bedrooms looked more inviting than those at the motel in the village, however. Philip tried out one of the beds, lying back. Ah. No harm in closing his eyes a bit . . .

It was dark when he awoke and of course at first he had no idea where he was. He sat up in panic. The clatter of a computer printer downstairs did not at first locate him in Wisconsin—it might have been Roger's printer in their house in Rye—but then he realized this was the home of the poet Webster. He yawned. Tomorrow they would get started eastward for home.

In the study, Roger was leaning against the side of the desk, waiting patiently as the computer printer piled up pages of text.

"Stealing a few gems?"

"The late poetry." But Roger did not seem joyous at the accusation.

"Anything wrong?"

Roger shrugged. "Poets change their styles from time to time. Webster's previous stages are clearly marked and much commented on. Apparently he had embarked on a quite new kind of poetry. I suppose with time I'll get used to it. Maybe earlier readers thought the Webster of the Elegies bore no relation to the poet who had published *Fragments*."

"How are they different?"

"These? In almost every way. Diction. Vocabulary. Theme. They scan very regularly and they rhyme. Webster had avoided rhyme in its obvious sense after the Elegies."

Once started, Roger could not stop, and his disquisition

continued as they shut down the computer, locked the cabinets and then the outer door. He paused for a moment as he stood beside the van and looked thoughtfully at the house and then turned to look across the field to the spot where the funeral pyre had blazed.

"I suppose these were the last scenes he saw."

"If he even noticed them."

"You're no poet, Philip."

Was this criticism? In any case, Roger continued talking about Webster's final poetic phase.

"As for the novella, I have to tell you it was reassuring to see it in his own hand. That was such a departure it would have been easy to believe it had been written by someone else."

Three days later, at home in Rye, enjoying the comfort and remoteness of their house, they were surprised to find Jane Clinton being interviewed on PBS.

6

STAYING WITH the nuns was strange. That had been her main misgiving about Albert's taking the job, the fact that Howard Webster had become a Catholic. Not much of one, by all accounts, but Jane wasn't sure she had ever known a Catholic who did not fall short of the ideal. Except for these nuns. But the fact that they fussed so over Felicia, an apparent benefactor of the convent, enabled Jane to suspect the sisters too of something less than perfection.

They did go on about Albert, and so did Felicia. The unpleasant realization came that the only interest she held for any of these people was the fact that she had been married to Albert. She tried to brush the thought away, to think of all the people who loved her for herself alone, but no names came to mind. Of course she hadn't been living in Madison long enough to get acquainted, let alone make friends. That had been the point of the move, after all, to be able to rub shoulders with real people rather than dodge wild dogs in the back country of Wisconsin.

She had Albert cremated when the body was released to her, a decision that saddened the nuns. Nonetheless, they held a memorial service for him too and there was nothing Jane could do but sit in the back of the squeaky-clean chapel, trying not to show her amazement. The nuns unpinned their veils and drooped them over their faces as they arrayed themselves on kneelers. Jane didn't realize at first that they were saying a rosary, but the repetition finally struck her and she knew that must be it. A rosary! She half wished Albert were alive so she could tell him this amazing story. She couldn't wait to tell it to somebody.

But who? Again Jane had the chilling thought that she was alone in the world indeed, without husband or family, without friends. She felt a twinge of panic go through her. It was as if she had died, not Albert. She would be glad when people stopped talking to her about him.

The first reporter came and she met him in a convent parlor, whispering to him before they got started that she wasn't a Catholic.

"Just your husband?"

"Albert wasn't either."

No response. How was she supposed to know he was from the Catholic diocesan paper? This time she was glad when he got going on Albert and Webster and living at the farm. He didn't seem to know of the move to Madison, and she saw no need to tell him. It would only complicate the story. When the director of the television program came, she agreed to be interviewed at the farm. Yes, she would be glad to point out some of the highlights of the home of the great poet Howard Webster.

It had its ironies, leading the cameraman about the farm, going out to where the poet had lit himself afire. Then they adjourned to the library and it was uncanny how Albert's spiel came to her lips and she chattered on and on about Webster's work.

"Can you tell us about the discovery of *The Leaden Echo*?"

"We weren't sure what it was at first, it was just a notebook, blue, hardboard covers . . ."

"A notebook?"

"Yes."

"I was referring to the handwritten manuscript of the novella."

Jane hesitated for only a moment. An old show-business maxim that the audience must be pleased seemed to guide her. Ah yes, the handwritten manuscript. All the holographs were a delight, but can you imagine what it was to come upon a work of prose fiction by Howard Webster?

"Tell us how you felt."

Jane looked into the camera. How practiced she was already. "It was a religious experience," she breathed. "Albert agreed. There was something almost holy about holding the text of a hitherto unsuspected Webster work."

1
PART TWO

WATCHING THE televised interview, Webster mimicked the fussy interviewer's voice, then the widow of the curator's, pressing the mute button so that his versions of their voices wouldn't have to compete with the originals, but he couldn't read their lips accurately enough so he turned the sound back on again. Jane was describing the excitement she and her husband had felt when they discovered the manuscript of *The Leaden Echo*.

Webster fell silent, all attention as the woman told the audience what a religious experience it had been to come upon the unknown story by the famous poet.

"The theme isn't religious, is it?" The interviewer leaned toward Jane, a secular Torquemada.

"Haven't you read it?"

Good girl. Answer a question with a question.

"Why do you call it a religious experience?"

Jane looked at him. "Have you ever been out early in the morning in autumn in the country when the fields are covered with fog? It's like walking through clouds, unreal, nothing seems substantial."

The interviewer was nodding vigorously long before she finished. Jane had made a convert of him. Now he understood what she meant by religion.

"Or the sound of a train at night, from far off . . ."

Quit while you're ahead, for God's sake, that guy never rode a train in his life, probably never noticed the wail they make.

But it was Jane Webster concentrated on. Like her husband, she had been living off his memory and he found he resented it. What she had said of the manuscript of the novella stuck in his mind and sure enough the interviewer brought her back to it by asking if there were other major discoveries she and her late husband had made.

"Who knows how many treasures there are to be discovered?" She turned and Webster felt she was looking directly at him. "But for me, there will always be the memory of coming upon that wonderfully written novella. I mean the script. Howard Webster had a distinctively elegant hand. We knew immediately it was his."

What kind of a con artist was she? Webster, knowing she could never have seen that manuscript in the circumstances she described, marveled at how persuasive she was. Unprepossessing lass, God knows, she reminded him of the gawky meatless kind who hung around after a reading, not really knowing what they wanted, unconsciously hoping lightning would strike. A time or two out of curiosity and compassion he had selected one of these wallflowers, hoping that under attention the girl would bloom. They hadn't. But having conferred their favors they were dangerously serious about the sequel. Better to stick with girls who were used to being pursued. But he wouldn't mind having a little talk with Jane.

Her very glibness with the interviewer turned her from an unattractive woman into a kind of menace. She could have seen the manuscript in recent days, after she came from Madison, but she knew that her story of the big discovery was a lie. Had she even wondered where such a manuscript had come from?

After Clinton slumped in his chair, asleep as Webster thought at first, in a diabetic coma as it would turn out, Webster had taken the copy of the novella and gone into the study where, at his desk, he had written out a fair copy of the novel on sheets of the paper on which he had always composed. It had taken him hours, but he was determined to do it. The more so after he took a break and tried to wake up Clinton and couldn't. Clinton had mentioned his diabetes. Webster's second wife had been diabetic and he recognized the symptoms. His first impulse was to get some food into the man, but he stopped himself. This was the solution. He went back to copying out the novella.

The point was to save his posthumous reputation, not to let the hoax Clinton had perpetrated provide an occasion to mock his achievement. It wasn't that he wanted to claim the novella as his own, to hell with the novella, but it had functioned to bring attention to all his work and for it to be revealed as a hoax would bring the bastards out of the wood-work. Webster knew critics, God did he know them. Just one of them would have to wonder aloud about the recent overestimation of Webster's early work and soon the whole pack would come baying after him and he would be consigned to an oblivion far deeper than that from which the novella had rescued him. He did not intend to let that happen.

It was nearly four in the morning when he finished. He had taken his time. The manuscript must not betray itself as hurried. He had deliberately introduced variations here and there, something to intrigue the critics. Who had authorized these changes when the sacred text was put into print? He might have left Clinton where he lay, having slipped from his chair onto the floor. There was no pulse. But he had vivid memories of how the events with Ober had really ended, not as in the novella, when presumably it was the author who resolved to end his own life. Because he was in the grips of those real events, he hoisted Clinton over his shoulder and toted him out to the barn where he threw a rope over the beam, tied it around Clinton's neck, and tugged him up until his feet swung free.

He had felt at the time that he was overdoing it. It was like writing lines he knew he'd change later. But he left Clinton hanging in the barn, deciding he could not undo what had happened to the poor devil's throat when he pulled the body up. He checked the house, centered the manuscript on the desk in the study, and left.

Taking Clinton's car was impulsive too, but he could not face the thought of walking down the lonely country road, heading for where he could catch a ride. He spent the night in Portage and then drove the car to Baraboo, wanting to see once more that town square that had so captivated him, with the great courthouse, the lawn cannon, every cliché in the book, but he had loved that town. He had sat in a Greek restaurant drinking muddy coffee and the opening of the first elegy had formed in his mind, starting as a smartass parody of Alan Tate, "Ode for the Union Survivors," but quickly refusing to be anything other than serious and elegiac, one of the best things he had ever written.

He parked Clinton's car, sat in the same Greek restaurant, ordered coffee and was overwhelmed by sadness as he considered what his life had been between beginning the first elegy and now. He had found his authentic voice at last, and he should have dedicated himself to it, swept everything else aside, stopped reading and making out and dissipating his energies for the cheap thrill of provincial applause, just write, now that he knew that what he wrote was good. That would have taken a moral strength he did not have. His poetry was all he had, that much he knew, but he could not arrange his life around that recognition.

The tinny red car parked up the street from where he sat disturbed him. He had to get rid of it. What a goddam dumb thing to fool around with a dead body like that, and then to steal the dead man's car. He began to wonder if anyone had seen him park it there. He stayed in the restaurant another twenty minutes, not sure he dared to get into that car and drive away. The Greyhound bus pulled in then, with Madison showing on its sign. Webster got aboard, leaving the little Toyota in Baraboo.

Now he sat in a motel watching Jane babble on about *The Leaden Echo* and increasingly she became a menace. Maybe she would never wonder where that manuscript had come from, but then again maybe she would. Somebody might put two and two together then and the night spent writing out that text would have been wasted. He would become a figure of fun, Clinton would be lionized in death . . . He couldn't bear the thought.

For the first time since returning from Sardinia he understood that there was nothing he could do as Howard Webster. He might just as well be literally dead. And he was running short of money too. The PBS interview ended with a segment with Felicia. Webster sat immobile, scarcely breathing, watching his daughter, listening to her voice, so eerily like her mother's. Jane might become lyrical about Howard Webster but it was obvious the poet's daughter would not.

"What does this do to the foundation?"

"I don't understand."

"Will the farm still be kept as a memorial?"

"Certainly. I shall be hiring a new curator . . ."

"With that unpaid commercial announcement, I have to close this interview," said the interviewer, casting a complicitous smile at the camera.

"I am not seeking applications," Felicia said sternly, every bit as literal as her mother. But it did deprive the interviewer of the last word, and that was something. There was no way in the world Webster would dare show up on Felicia's doorstep. But her talk of a new curator gave him the semblance of a plan. He would buy a motorbike and head back to the village, waiting for the new curator to be chosen.

2

A CALL from New Orleans took Philip away for a week and although he called Roger every day he was absorbed in the case in hand, persuading a runaway daughter to return to St. Louis, a job that entailed too many late nights in the French Quarter. The girl, if a twenty-three-year-old young woman can be called a girl, had decided to try her luck offering to do portraits of tourists and her lack of talent and one or two irate customers did not dissuade her. Philip figured it was only a matter of time. Meanwhile he enjoyed the sunny square in front of St. Louis Cathedral, sat several times for his own portrait, threw away all but one, a charcoal-and-chalk that flattered him sufficiently, and kept his eye on Hazel, his subject. If things got desperate he would sit for her, but for the nonce there was no point in confronting her in the flesh. He had talked to her on the phone several times since arriving and locating her, but she had no idea what he looked like.

After he dropped Hazel off in St. Louis, he flew home to

Rye where Roger welcomed him with pizza and beer, the former delivered piping hot, the latter cold from the fridge.

"They found the car."

Philip munched on pizza and looked at Roger.

"It was in Baraboo of all places. Inevitably one imagines there is significance to that."

Philip had no idea what Roger was talking about. The excursion to Wisconsin was only a past event now, a not very satisfying excursion. Gradually Roger made it clear that he was speaking of Clinton's car that had been unaccountably missing when he was found dead. It had turned up in Baraboo, a town that had occasioned a series of Webster's poems. Now that he understood, Philip saw no reason why this should interest him.

"Who put it there, Philip?"

"Whoever stole it."

"Who would steal that battered Toyota?"

"Lots of kids if the keys were left in it as they were."

"You don't think it means anything?"

"Not to me."

"I wish we'd stayed."

"Roger, my job was done."

"I talked with Ned Bunting on the telephone. That's how I found out about the car."

"Why did you call him?"

Philip had never doubted the genuineness of Roger's interest in the work of Howard Webster but since returning home Roger had resumed his regular routine, half the day at the computer, the other half reading. A collection of fragments of pre-Socratic philosophers, edited by Kirk and Raven, held his attention during the first few days after Wisconsin, seemingly a departure from the literary emphasis, but it was the themes of Webster's early poems that had sent Roger back to the origins of Greek philosophy where the poet had found some of his more persistent themes. He went on to Homer, the *Iliad* and *Odyssey*, and then began a systematic study of the English translations made of these two works over the years.

"Remember 'On First Looking into Chapman's Homer'?" Roger asked. Philip did not answer. "This is Chapman." He held up the book he was reading.

"Who did Chapman play for?"

Roger's laughter was incommensurate with the poor humor of the remark but an index of the childlike simplicity that accompanied Roger's mental capacities.

"Bunting said he would tell the Wisconsin Bureau of Investigation to check the car for prints if they hadn't already done so."

"Good idea."

But remote. Philip no longer cared much what happened in distant Wisconsin. He spent much of his first day back working in the yard, raking and bagging leaves, getting the flower beds ready for winter. The bracing fall air made him believe he almost longed for winter, with the countryside white with snow and the dogs romping about in it like puppies. He used the blower to clean out the drive. Better that than this dull time of naked branches, the fallen leaves losing their color, the chill in the air unrelieved by compensatory natural beauty. He could always fly south when the winter got him down.

"There were prints in the car," Roger said when Philip came inside.

"Of course there were."

Roger kept tapping away at his computer keyboard, writing a letter on E-mail to an Icelandic correspondent.

"Clinton's. And Jane's. Some of Howard Webster's too." He swung away from the screen. "Isn't that eerie? A person's prints showing up long after they're dead. Mine on these keys would survive me, but for how long, I wonder."

"Look it up."

Roger smiled. It was an old joke, what Philip had said to Roger years ago when his little brother would not stop asking questions. Before Roger was revealed as a genius, Philip had felt reasonably intelligent, he was intelligent, but under the onslaught of Roger's relentless questioning he felt like the village idiot. Telling Roger to "look it up" had proved to be his best defense.

"There were none of the thief."

"I'm not surprised."

Philip was home a week before responding to another call on his 800 number, this one from Cincinnati, the theft of some sacred vessels from a church.

"Catholic?"

"Sacred Heart."

"It's got to be."

Philip waited, wondering if Roger would want to come along. His fat brother's conversion to Catholicism as a graduate student at Princeton had come out of the blue, triggered by reading Chaucer.

"Chaucer! That's pretty raunchy stuff, isn't it?"

"Sinners on pilgrimage. Like ourselves."

It was as close as Roger got to suggesting Philip might want to join him in his religious conversion. The change had been from a vague agnosticism to a wholehearted acceptance of a list of beliefs and practices. Philip had given up trying to understand it. Sundays he carted Roger into town for Mass while he himself picked up the Sunday papers, put gas in the van, had a cup of coffee in the old depot that had been converted into a mall.

But it was Chaucer's remarks in later life about the *Tales* that had first struck Roger, then the realization that "The Miller's Tale" had a kind of innocence to it because of a background that was all but invisible to the modern reader. This broadened into a theory about the obstacles that stood between the great literature of the West and the modern reader. C.S. Lewis, it turned out, had had similar thoughts and within a week Roger had read everything Lewis had written.

"I don't like his fiction much, but the rest of it is wonderful."

In Howard Webster he had found, oddly enough, a fellow convert more to his liking. The poet's multiple marriages, his doubtful observance of the demands of his new faith, the flow of scandalous rumors, did nothing to shake Roger's devotion.

"His imagination is baptized, Philip. That's the important thing." But he added, "If one is a poet, that is."

Roger certainly excused himself from none of the demands of Catholicism, sighed over dissident theologians, liked to speak of the faithful as in diaspora, the institutions built up in the preconciliar heyday rapidly becoming indistinguishable from their secular or previously secularized counterparts. But aren't there still Catholic universities? "Is Princeton Presbyterian?"

3

"WHAT HAVE you done with those letters?"

"Letters?"

"Frank, don't lie. You've been lying to me for years but not now. You've taken the letters from the metal trunk in the attic."

She stood before him, fists dug into her hips, feet planted; this was war. Was it deliberate that the light was behind her and he could not see her face?

"Your father's letters?"

She shifted. Even now in her anger she could not bear to mention her father's name.

"I'm getting them appraised."

"You . . . are . . . getting . . . them . . . appraised." Each word was said separately, as if to make certain the Recording Angel was getting it all.

"His letters have become extremely valuable and . . ."

"What has the value of his letters got to do with you! I will not sell those letters. I would rather burn them."

"Felicia, I am simply making an inquiry." No point in telling her what Hollander hoped to get for the letters. Frank scarcely believed the man himself. But of course it was through Hector that he knew of those expectations.

She collapsed in a chair across the table from him. He sipped his coffee as if this were a perfectly normal breakfast conversation. In a way it was. He seemed to be in a permanently vulnerable position with Felicia. He had told her of losing money, mentioning only half the sum involved, incredulous himself that he had really and truly frittered away such amounts. That she had discovered the absence of the letters so soon startled him, but the guilt and shame that followed were familiar friends.

"Is Hector involved?"

He laughed. "Once burned, twice shy."

After a moment's silence, she said, "Then he is."

"What does it matter who acts for us?"

"For us!"

He had spoken without rhetorical intent, but now he seized upon this inclusive view of his fate. "Felicia, we are in very deep financial difficulties. I am desperate. I have to get out from under this debt. There is no point in working now, everything I earn is already owed."

"Don't exaggerate with me."

"Exaggerate? God, I wish I were. Felicia, I am truly frightened. It's not even clear I could salvage anything by declaring bankruptcy. They could move in and take everything, the house, the cars, the furniture. The letters."

The effect on her of the full truth of his situation, of their situation, was profound. He should have been honest with her before, but before he had always been looking over the debris of one failure to the shimmering hope of a new possibility, one that would more than make up for earlier failures. But in the case of the letters, Frank had seen them only as a means of crawling out of debt. A packet of old letters in the attic written by a hated father seemed a small price to pay to get back to Square One again, to sever all ties with Hector, to begin to enjoy the success he had and stop dreaming of what he didn't have.

"You're serious."

He took her hand. "I have never been more serious in my life. I am truly afraid."

"And the letters will solve everything?"

"Maybe not everything."

He sat with bowed head, wanting to drink his coffee, but retaining the posture of a penitent. He had told her the whole thing at last, there was nothing held back, it could never be worse than this. His stupidity had been multiplied beyond the point of absurdity. An intelligent, successful man had squandered hundreds of thousands of dollars and now a few allegedly valuable letters represented his hedge against bankruptcy.

"What in the name of God did you plan to do?"

Again she stood silhouetted against the sunlit french doors.

"This."

"This?"

"Talk to you about it."

"Why?"

"Your father is our only salvation, Felicia."

"No!"

"Whether you like it or not, he was a great man. His work is bringing in royalties greater than anything he earned while he was alive."

She actually clamped her hands over her ears and began to sway where she stood, but Frank went on, what he had to say meant to console himself as well as inform her.

Felicia had turned over everything her father had left to the foundation which, as it turned out now, was fine. His debtors could not get at it. When Frank visited him Cannon had sat silently making faces as he explained to the lawyer

the fix he'd gotten himself into. He could never admit the
dimensions of his folly to Alex, his own lawyer, which meant
that he had defrauded not only the government but made
his lawyer an unwitting partner in it. Cannon was different.
It was made easier because he portrayed Hector as the hero
of this tragicomedy, a friend who had been betrayed by a
third party.

"And you want to help him. Why?" asked Cannon.

"He's a friend."

"That's not a good reason for lending this amount of
money to someone with a track record for failure."

"You may be right. What I need to know is the chance
Felicia would have to reclaim some of the assets she turned
over to the foundation."

Cannon sat back as if he had been punched in the
stomach.

"Reclaim?"

"Take back. Realize the kind of money I'm talking about."

Cannon would not have been a lawyer if he didn't give
Frank a lecture on the setup of tax-free foundations, the
provisions that had been made to ensure that people didn't
slip money into such foundations only to withdraw it later,
having in the meantime escaped paying taxes on it.
Legislators, well schooled as they were in the predatory arts,
had written the law to protect such foundations from opportunists like themselves.

"There must be a way. Find a way, Gerry."

"This poor devil we're talking about, Frank, it's you, isn't
it?"

"Would you work harder at this if you thought so?"

Cannon smiled and squeezed his elbow. "Trust me."

It was the first remark that made Frank wonder if he hadn't
added a new mistake to the pile of those already made. Trust
Gerry Cannon? When Felicia had first come up with the
idea of creating the Webster Foundation, it had seemed so

insubstantial a project that Frank had only raised an eyebrow at her involving Cannon, the boyhood friend of her father. The lawyer would fit right in with so ephemeral a thing. Cannon as officer of the fund? Why not? The amount of money originally involved was risible, the property in rural Wisconsin, the royalties, Webster's retirement plan. But then had come *The Leaden Echo* and suddenly everything Howard Webster had left turned to gold. Who could blame Cannon if his sense of self-importance rose with the value of the fund? Perhaps he imagined that his own stewardship had something to do with the altered fortunes of the Webster Foundation. But Cannon's suggestion that Frank trust him had the opposite effect and he went out to his car wondering if Gerry Cannon could indeed be trusted with what now amounted to several million dollars. Were the laws written tightly enough to prevent a trustee from skimming from all that tax-free money?

He stopped at Hector's office but his partner was not there. The silent partner had been invisible too since Frank turned over to him those Howard Webster letters. He sat at Hector's desk, piled high with correspondence, brochures, file folders, books, magazines, Styrofoam cartons that had held Big Macs, an assortment of paper cups, their insides stained by the coffee that had evaporated from them. Frank turned the chair to the left and flicked on Hector's computer and it groaned into life. He called up the directory of the hard disk and was mildly amused by the scatological terms Hector had used as names for his files. He called up Turd and found to his annoyance that it contained a memo Hector had written to Frank complaining of the demise of a half-forgotten direct-mail scheme. Did the file name designate the project or the addressee?

But his thoughts kept going back to Cannon and to Felicia's manifest distrust of the lawyer. That was when he remembered the detective from Rye, New York, the Webster

Foundation had brought in to find the missing manuscript that wasn't missing. But he was more concerned about Hector. He found the phone book, cleared a place for it on the desk, and turned to the index of the *Yellow Pages*. Detectives. *See Investigators, private.* At the indicated page in a small box was the legend "Philip Knight 1-800-321-0692." Frank dialed the number having rehearsed a story to the effect that the Webster Foundation had further need of Knight's services.

4

WINKLE TELEPHONED and Phasic wrote and there were other applications as well, Webster scholars and assorted academic opportunists drawn by the prospect of the sinecure in rural Wisconsin that had been left open by the death of Albert Clinton. Felicia prepared a form letter to thank applicants and assure them that their inquiries would be taken with the utmost seriousness. But it was Skye's letter that caught her attention. Him she wrote personally, suggesting that he come to Milwaukee. Two days later he telephoned.

"When can you come?"

"I'm here now."

"In Milwaukee?"

"Yes."

She had written him in Tulsa. He must have taken a red-eye out of Oklahoma as soon as he received her note. This was promising.

"Where are you staying?"

"I'm calling from the airport."

She told him to meet her at the Hayes and arrived early to wait in the lobby. She wanted a first look at him. When the airport van arrived three people got out, a middle-aged couple and a short man wearing cowboy boots, jeans and a tan corduroy jacket with patches on the elbows. That would be Skye. Felicia remained where she was, watching him cross the lobby, an overnight pack slung over his shoulder, peering about him through bottle-bottom glasses. Skye had described himself as a paleographer with experience in cataloguing. Felicia had called her congressman who called the Library of Congress and two hours later Felicia learned that Skye had been fired from a cataloguing project at Princeton, resigned actually, so that charges would not be brought. He had been in contact with an Italian art historian once involved in a theft from the Ambrosian Library in Milan and there was good reason to suspect that they had been conspiring to remove several Dürer engravings from the library.

An announcement was heard, asking Mrs. Leamon to pick up any lobby phone for a message. Skye leaned against the desk, looking about, anxious to see who responded to the message. Felicia lit a cigarette and waited. Skye turned and began to chat with the clerk, from time to time looking over his shoulder. He was beginning to worry that he had mistaken the message. After another cigarette, Felicia rose and walked rapidly toward Skye.

"Bernard Skye? Felicia Leamon. Have you checked in?"

"Should I?"

Felicia summoned the clerk. "There is a room reserved in the name of the Webster Foundation. Would you put Mr. Skye in it?"

Already she was sure that Skye was the person she wanted as curator of her father's papers.

At lunch he refused the offer of a drink but when she ordered a Bloody Mary, said he would have a Scotch and water after all.

"It *is* after twelve." His smile came and went.

"Tell me about yourself."

His credentials, if he could be believed, were excellent. He had taken his doctorate in Munich where he had studied with Bischoff. He did not mention Princeton when he told her where he had worked, conveying the impression that he still taught at Cal Tech, the position from which he had gone to Princeton.

"Why Tulsa?"

He pulled a long face. "My father is ill. Terminally."

His father had been dead five years. "What do you know of Howard Webster?"

He put down his glass carefully. "Nothing."

"Why did you apply for the job?"

"Why did you invite me to Milwaukee?"

They sat in silence for a minute, looking at one another, then Felicia signaled the waiter. "Another Scotch and water, please."

Eventually they ate lunch, although by then it was clear that Skye would have been content to while away the afternoon drinking Scotch. She told him she knew about his difficulties at Princeton.

"Tell me about the Webster Foundation."

"Howard Webster was my father."

"What does the job involve?"

She told him she would take him to the farm the following day and show him on the spot what the curator did.

"Am I hired?"

"I'll tell you tomorrow, after we've been to the farm."

He sat back. "Is something wrong with the place?"

"No. It is a bit isolated."

"That wouldn't bother me. If the work is interesting."

She had not told Frank of her plan, not because she was ashamed of it, but rather because she felt he did not deserve to know that she had hit upon a way to rescue them financially and get out of the clutches of Cannon. She had taken the precaution of removing from the files of the Milwaukee office the printouts Clinton had sent her of the papers he had already catalogued. Her plan was simple. With the help of Skye she would remove the bulk of the papers from the farm, store them elsewhere and stage a great discovery of papers that would be hers and not the foundation's. This would give her freedom of movement to regain control over her father's literary remains.

Could she steal from herself? Legally, perhaps, given the existence of the Webster Foundation and her bequest of all known papers, but those holdings were morally hers and with Skye's help, she would reclaim the bulk of them. Skye seemed to have the moral character, or lack of it, she needed in a co-conspirator.

The following day, driving westward, she answered Skye's questions, curious to know what they would be. He had not heard of the manner of her father's death and listened openmouthed while she told him.

"He set himself on fire!"

"Yes."

"My God."

"Chances are he was drunk at the time."

"You mean it was an accident?"

"Oh no. But it was clear from his notebook that he had been drinking heavily. A man had been staying with him, someone with whom to drink, but they had fought and he was alone and he was suddenly overwhelmed by the futility of his life. His phrase."

"Drunk or sober, that's the damnedest thing I ever heard of."

She was surprised he hadn't heard of it before, or hadn't checked up on Howard Webster and read of it, but he was obviously surprised. Shocked. Horrified.

"The first curator committed suicide."

"C'mon."

"I'm serious."

If she had not been sure of him, that he needed this job, she might have skipped the gory details about Clinton.

"A detective I hired to find the missing manuscript felt that Clinton had not committed suicide."

"You said he was found hanging."

"The detective's theory was that he had been strung up after he died."

"You're making this up."

"No, he was. Knight. The detective. Or rather his brother."

Skye began to shake his head, stopping only to drag on his cigarette. "How many people applied for this job?"

"Eight, not counting yourself."

"How many have you interviewed?"

"You're the first."

"Why?"

"Because of your Princeton experience."

"I don't understand."

"You will in time."

It was important that he have some inkling of what he would be expected to do, but now was not the time for details. She wanted him settled in, used to solitude, even more amenable than he already was.

She stopped in the village and introduced him to Ned Bunting and the Thorwalds.

"They found his car," Bunting said. "Clinton's."

"Where?"

"Baraboo."

"Jane will be glad for that."

Bunting rejected the idea that local kids had taken the car for a joyride and abandoned it in Baraboo, but she advanced this for Skye's benefit, not the sheriff's. It occurred to her that Knight's fantastic notion of how Clinton had died required someone to hang up the already dead Clinton. She wanted Skye pliable, but not scared out of his wits.

He wanted to stop at the liquor store but she suggested he first see what supplies there were at the farm.

"Nice," he said, when she turned in the drive and advanced slowly toward the house. It did have a pleasant look, she thought, seeing it as if for the first time. The place had always appeared to her through the lens of her feeling toward her father, but now it had the look of promise. That she should now want to reclaim her father's papers seemed a trick she was playing on him, she wasn't quite sure why.

Skye had assured her on the phone that he was adept with the computer and it was largely to find out if this was true that she had come with him to the farm. He settled at the keyboard and began to examine the files. Meanwhile Felicia opened a file of as yet uncatalogued material and began to fill her briefcase.

"He made a beginning," Skye said, after a minute.

"I've seen the printout."

"Any idea what percentage that amounts to?"

"Can that stuff be erased?"

He turned to look at her. "He must have made a backup."

"But it could be done?"

"Don't even think of it."

"Erase it."

He laughed, but stopped when he saw she was serious.

"I mean it. I want you to start from scratch."

"But . . ."

After a moment, he shrugged. "You're the boss." But he lifted his fingers from the keyboard. "Let's talk about my salary."

5

THE NOTE was in her mailbox but it hadn't been mailed, an envelope with Aran written on it and inside the note: *I will telephone.*

Unsigned, but God in heaven what need was there for a signature with handwriting as distinctive as his? She read the note on the way upstairs in the elevator and the hair on the back of her neck responded to the incredible thrill of it. A hoax. It had to be a hoax. The elevator arrived at her floor, the door slid open, but Aran did not get out. The thought of picking up the telephone and hearing his voice. . .

She punched the button, went down again and outside and into her car and just drove. At stoplights, she glanced again and again at the note, hopeful that some clue as to its fraudulence would be revealed, but each time it looked even more like the handwriting of Howard Webster.

The late Howard Webster. Her dead husband who had set himself afire and been reduced to ashes. He must have been drunk, that was the only explanation. Such an exit was the kind he could dream of, but actually to put into execution, no. She knew Howard Webster for a self-indulgent, self-loving, arrogant, lovable sonofabitch. The only harm he had ever caused himself was the result of the pell-mell pursuit of pleasure.

She smiled at the impossible thought that this note could mean that those crazy years she had spent with Howard were not altogether over, that somehow . . . Crazy.

In a dimly lit lounge where she stopped for a drink, Aran went through the thing carefully. Howard Webster was dead and therefore incapable of putting a note in her mailbox telling her he would telephone. Nonetheless, she had received a note in his handwriting with that message. Someone could learn to mimic his handwriting, forgers do that sort of thing all the time, don't they? And voices too can be imitated. Of course. Rich Little became dozens of people. A determined person could learn to sound like Howard Webster for purposes of a phone conversation. And of course that was the reason for all the indirectness. In person, she would recognize the hoax.

She lit another cigarette as if to clear her thoughts. She found her reasoning almost unwelcome. Confess it, in the elevator, when she first read the note, she had believed. Howard was still alive, he had come and left the note, he would call. How vulnerable she was. She wanted so much to think that he would come back and defend her interests that she would go to meet the mimic halfway.

During the past years, Aran had felt unjustly dealt with as, if not the widow, then the most recent wife of Howard Webster. Granted that, right afterward, when she read the news of his fiery death, she had in the privacy of her own room let out a little cheer of triumph. The bastard was dead at last. He had all but thrown her out and given her nothing except the dubious honor of being able to call herself Mrs. Webster. Not much of a job description that, though several aspiring poets had come sniffing around, perhaps hoping that something of her late husband might rub off on them if she let them get close enough. What she had done was go back to work at the *Journal*, taking up where she had left off some years back when she had gone out one fateful day to interview the great poet Howard Webster, in retirement on his farm north of Madison.

"Aran?" he had said.

"As in islands."

"No man is an island."

"I'm no man."

But he had already noticed that. He adopted a brogue, of course, he was a wonderful mimic, and offered her a drop and it was Jameson's but why not? They sat in the library and he interviewed her, wanting to know about growing up in County Clare and had she seen Yeats's tower. Of course she had, she lied, and so had he, he lied, and so it went, a few drops more from time to time, and if she got out of there unbedded on that first visit it was only a matter of time and they both knew it. She had already formed in her mind the thought that the only way he was going to get her into bed was to make her his first Catholic wife. And so he did, though not quite in that order.

To this day she could just sit still and close her eyes and relive that wonderful time, wonderful and awful; he was a terrible drunk, worse than an Irish drunk, a drunk like her father and brothers had been, a morning, noon and night drinker with never a moment when it was certain the mind was clear. She did not want to think that he'd not been sober when they married. But that had been his claim when he'd had the gall to apply for an annulment. In the end he had to settle for a civil divorce and that had been the basis of Aran's claim. They had remained married, Howard and she; what God had put together let no man put asunder.

Asunder was a word he had loved and he played with it as if it were a woman.

Asunder her man
so sundered was she
she cried out in wonder
I love my asunder.

And other ribald doggerel that he spun for her by the hour. They honeymooned right there on the farm, in the great echoing house, going from bedroom to bedroom, scarcely ever asunder. That was to be the problem. He thought of her as only a roll in the hay, not a wife, but despite the difference in age, she had wanted children.

"I've got a child."

He meant Felicia, a grown-up woman as old as Aran. "I said a baby, not a child."

Oh, the idea appealed to him, she could see that right off, the speculative look as he imagined the reaction. It would dispel the notion that he was an old man, waiting to die on his farm, his life and work effectively over. When she came to interview him, that had been her notion as well. What a surprise to learn that he saw his career as in a temporary trough, he would soon come into his own again. Had he really believed that? She hadn't, try as she could, but he had been right and she had been wrong. Even if he had to be dead before his career came right again.

How she had learned to hate her erstwhile friend Felicia since, trying to talk sense to the woman, after all, his wife should get *something* from the bonanza Howard's work now proved to be. Felicia listened impassively, with apparent interest, and at first Aran had actually hoped that Howard's daughter agreed. Howard's daughter! She had hated her father and was determined to institutionalize his failure, that was the point of the foundation. Aran had realized this when she saw Felicia's reaction to the enormous success of *The Leaden Echo.*

"I always believed in that book," Aran had said.

Felicia ignored this claim to have known of the novella,

whether because she knew it to be false or because she didn't care.

"My lawyer's argument would be that I deserve at least as much a split as courts have been awarding in palimony suits."

Felicia looked remarkably unthreatened. This is what Aran meant to suggest to a lawyer if she decided to consult one. Lee Marvin had gotten it in the chops, so why not Howard Webster?

"There's enough for both of us, Felicia."

"I wouldn't take a nickel." It was a hiss as much as a statement and Aran began to see what she was up against.

Aran had never gotten a nickel, she had never seen a lawyer, she had gone on working and tried to forget the pain and delight of being the wife of Howard Webster.

After a second drink, in the Ladies, Aran studied the note in the lemony lights of the makeup mirror. She lifted her eyes and looked at a woman who would give anything if Howard was still alive and wanted to see her.

6

BERNARD SKYE realized Felicia thought he was a crook but of course that is not how he thought of himself. Princeton? The team of paleographers he had belonged to fought as paleographers always did, the bickering petty, backbiting, meanspirited and constant, and it did not help that Imelda Bose, the senior paleographer, was a misanthrope who regarded males as an evolutionary failure. How else explain those undeveloped male breasts? Skye was the first straight male she had hired and that was because he misled her about his sexual orientation, as it was delicately called. As for the supposed plot with Mario, it was just drunken talk, though Skye had convinced himself that it was possible to remove the two engravings. Trying to get a price on them had been the mistake, though the dealer testified that it was simply an idle inquiry, there had been no question whatsoever of buying the engravings, but then the dealer was supposed to be in on it, so what good was his word? Skye agreed to resign with the understanding that the accusation would not become part of his record. What an ass he had been to trust

Imelda. His applications had been ignored and his phone calls inquiring about them went unanswered until finally an old friend told him that Imelda had effectively blackballed him. He had gone home to Tulsa to brood when the same friend called to tell him of the Howard Webster opening.

"Not much to do, and it's out in the sticks, still . . ."

But Skye came to enjoy the solitude. There was booze aplenty and fresh air and time to ponder the enigmatic Felicia, the daughter of the poet. His first task had been to acquaint himself with the writer whose papers stood in locked file cabinets in the study. He had not yet been given keys to the cabinets, but he had taken the precaution to make copies of the computer files before erasing them from the hard disk. Felicia seemed genuinely innocent of the computer and did not suspect the disks he filled with data from the hard disk. Before she left he was able to show her that the hard disk was erased.

"Good."

"Now that I've undone that, what shall I do?"

She picked up her bulging briefcase. "First I want you to make a record of my father's books."

"On the computer?"

"Yes."

Did she know of the card catalogue her father had made of his books? It certainly simplified his work once he'd checked the shelves against the cards and saw that they matched. He began the undemanding task of entering the data from the cards onto the computer, devoting several hours a day to it, and then settling on the porch in gloves and jacket and cap, holding a beer, smoking a cigar and looking out over what he came to think of as his property. These sessions on the porch gave him time to ponder the strange behavior of Felicia Webster Leamon. She visited frequently as he settled in, each time filling her briefcase from the file cabinets. She looked him in the eye and spoke nonstop as she did this, as if she were not doing what she was, or was engaged in some forbidden activity, but he could not for the life of him imagine what it was. The thought occurred to him that it was he who interested her, that she had hired him because she found him attractive. Whatever he himself knew to be his accomplishments and training, Imelda had cast such a pall over it that he could not believe that somehow Felicia saw past his clouded record to the first-rate paleographer he was. Only she had no need for a paleographer. The job at the farm could have been done by any dolt, a low-grade librarian, even Ned Bunting.

"Stay out of the barn," Ned had told him a dozen times if he had told him once. This was a punch line that always doubled Ned up in a wheezing laugh. The reference was to Skye's predecessor. Funny. Still the wags in the village were all there was by way of company, and evenings he went in town for a beer, usually ate at the diner where Mrs. Blatz provided starchy food for any traveler who had been improvident enough to find himself at day's end in the village. That was where he met Ober.

Bearded, in his sixties, wearing a beret, he had held his mug of coffee in two hands and hunched forward over the counter. He nodded without looking up when Skye said hello. Skye moved over to the stool next to the stranger.

"Never saw you around before."

"Just got in."

"Don't tell me you were headed for this place."

"You the fellow works out at the Webster farm?"

Skye looked toward Mrs. Blatz but she scuttled into the kitchen.

"That's me."

"My name's Ober."

"Skye."

"That's what she said." He meant Mrs. Blatz. "The name Ober mean anything to you?"

"Should it?"

"The Leaden Echo."

Skye waited but then a bell rang, that was the title of one of Webster's works.

"I'm that Ober."

"No kidding."

Ober laughed. "You don't know, do you?"

"Tell me."

But Mrs. Blatz arrived with his dinner and while he was eating Ober slid off his stool and left.

"Who's he?" Skye asked Mrs. Blatz.

"I don't know."

It didn't seem right, her telling someone more of a stranger here than he was who he was. The only explanation seemed to be that she didn't know who Ober was. Skye thought of asking Bunting but decided against it. That night he read *The Leaden Echo.*

Nuts used to claim to be Napoleon. Skye figured the stranger in the diner had decided to become a character in a story. Weird. But the mail and the occasional phone call had made him aware that the fans of late literary greats tended to take a very possessive attitude toward the object of their affection. Skye began to talk to the photograph of Howard Webster that looked at him from the wall of the study for help. What he didn't know about Webster he made up. Felicia came by and took away another load of material from a file cabinet. He told her the books were coming along fine.

"Good."

She reacted as she might to being told he'd been making snowmen in the yard. The first snowfall had turned the farm into a wholly new place. Beautiful. Skye couldn't believe what a deal he had fallen into. Room and board and a good salary besides. There had to be a catch. But he couldn't figure out what it might be. He didn't mention Ober to Felicia. Why bother her with the story of some nut?

The following day, Ober came up the drive, on foot.

7

THE PICKUP pulled to the side of the road and the driver, toothless, chewed an imaginary cud.

"You sure?"

Webster pushed at his chin whiskers with the heel of his hand, leaning forward to look up the driveway at his house. "This is the place."

"That place is spooked."

Webster, about to open the door, hesitated. "Oh?"

"The last two people lived there, don't. Dead. One lit himself on fire like a goddam bonfire."

"I heard about that."

"I'm going on to the village."

"No, I'll get out here."

Webster had caught the ride at an exit ramp of I-90 and the driver hadn't spoken five words until now.

"You some kind of relative?"

Webster leaned in the open window of the door he had just shut. "Insurance investigator." He winked conspiratorially and was twenty feet up the driveway before the pickup drove away, seeming to accelerate toward the village. It was dumb to want to *épater les rustiques* like that. The man would spread the story far and wide. Not that the farm wasn't already firmly a part of local mythology.

The man who stepped off the porch was Skye.

The trouble with Wolfe was that he got everything wrong, flamboyantly wrong, but wrong nonetheless. It was because we *can* go home, again and again, that the past does not lose its grip on us. Coming up his driveway, Webster felt he was reliving the first time he had seen the place and hundreds of other times as well, including the most recent. Erase Skye and he could imagine Aran waiting for him there.

Aran had not recognized him when she finally agreed to meet him, in a saloon, where else? The note she had believed, more or less, and his voice on the phone, but she came in and sat at the table next to his without so much as a glance in his direction, sitting so she could watch the door. After fifteen minutes, she became nervous, but she continued to nurse her drink, as if she had resolved to be clear-minded for this.

He got up, pulled out a chair and sat next to her. "Hello, Aran."

"Do I know you?"

" 'Did bone know flesh?' "

From the elegy he had dedicated to her. She recognized it but it did not have the effect he had intended. Her shoulders sank and she looked at him, a tragic mask.

"Are you the one who telephoned?"

He took off the beret and tilted his chin. Nothing. He covered the beard with his hand. She wanted to recognize him, he could see that, but she refused to kid herself.

"I'm Howard, Aran."

"Please. Your hoax worked, up to a point, but let's just stop it right now."

He could see her difficulty. He had thought of it himself. Handwriting and voices can be imitated, a man's work can be memorized by anyone, but he had not dreamt he had changed so much.

"You don't recognize me."

"Please."

"Death is hard on a person." He leaned toward her. "On the second day, in the front bedroom, two in the afternoon, you and I and a bottle of dago red." She narrowed her eyes and peered at him.

"Anyone could have . . ."

"Anyone?" He began to unbutton his shirt.

"What are you doing!"

"One swallow docsn't make a spring." He had two, one over each breast. The corners of her mouth trembled. He got his shirt unbuttoned and exposed a swallow.

"My God," she breathed.

He laid his hand on hers and said, "Sweetheart, just shut up and listen. This is a very crazy story."

He had been older than Aran when they married, but not old. Now he was old, almost unrecognizable to her after bumming around in the Sardinian sun for more than a year, no longer what he had been as a lover, but that added a kind of tenderness to their reunion. She lay beside him, propped on an elbow, tracing the tattooed swallows with her long-nailed finger. She had covered his mouth, shocked, when he told her now she knew how Mary Magdalene had felt.

"Don't be blasphemous."

"I was referring to her alleged profession."

She slapped him. A good fight had always been the prelude to their best times together, and this, while not much compared to the standards of yore, was the first lovemaking he had engaged in since his death.

"How could you pull such a stunt?"

"Aran, all I did was walk away."

"After lighting fire to that poor tramp."

"He was dead. Do you think the county would have given him a better funeral? It was a corporal act of mercy." She seemed pleased that he remembered his catechism. "Like sleeping with you." She slapped him again but he grabbed her wrist. He didn't want her to make a habit of that.

Telling her of his chosen exile, of the solitude he had known in Sardinia, he realized how much he had needed to speak frankly with someone who had known him.

"I learned of my posthumous fame a month ago when I picked up an old magazine in a barber shop."

"And decided not to get a haircut?"

"I like it long."

"So do I."

Distractions, distractions, but what the hell, the simple pleasures of the flesh were welcome after such abstinence. Two in one flesh, still married in her eyes, and a good thing. Aran's story about Felicia didn't really surprise him so if he was going to profit at all from his good fortune without rising from the dead he was going to have to rely on Aran.

"Why not just let everyone know you're alive?"

"And be welcomed back with open arms?"

She thought about it. "What do you care what people say?"

"Why bother at all. Being dead has its compensations."

Now, the new curator came toward him, wearing half a smile, obviously glad to have a visitor.

"I'm Bernard Skye. Welcome to the home of Howard Webster."

"We met in the village a while back."

"Oh?"

"My name's Ober."

His eyes grew round. "Sure. As in the book."

1

MRS. THORWALD sent on the *Village Ear* as well as clippings from Milwaukee and Madison papers on the assumption that the Knights had developed a permanent affection for her part of Wisconsin. Of course Roger had brought out the mother in the childless wife of the local physician, pharmacist and deputy coroner. The news of the accident in which Jane Clinton lost her life was a routine item in the Madison paper, reprinted in the village weekly with the cryptic addendum that readers might remember Mrs. Clinton as the wife of the late curator of the Howard Webster Library.

"Can you imagine?" Mrs. Thorwald asked rhetorically in her accompanying letter. "Two young people dead in the prime of life and that's all Leon Kelzer can think to write about it. Why, the thing is a tragedy, a theme worthy of Howard Webster himself."

There was more, Mrs. Thorwald making up for her distant correspondent in Rye what was wanting in the unction of Leon Kelzer, editor of the weekly. But it was the brevity of the account of the accident that struck Roger and Philip.

No other fatalities or injuries were mentioned. Did that mean it was a single-car accident? The only detail was that it had happened on I-90 North. A patch of ice on an overpass? A reckless semi that had frightened her into a fatal turn of the wheel? Dozing off while driving? There were so many possibilities to tease the mind when the account told them nothing.

"Why guess," Philip said. "I'll call WBI."

The elation Roger had felt upon hearing that Philip would pursue the matter of Jane's death diminished at the mention of Verda. It had been Roger's fear that Philip's affection for Verda when she had worked for him in Manhattan would blossom into a permanent thing that would become a wedge between the brothers. Quite apart from the fact that working with someone is the very opposite of an aphrodisiac, Verda had been rendered cynical by a failed marriage and Philip had never been able to feel tender toward a woman as tall as himself. A year ago Verda had been of help to him in a Minneapolis case that had spilled over into Eau Claire.

"Funny you should ask," Verda said when he got through to her.

"Why?"

"Nobody else has. That's the saddest thing about some deaths. There are no mourners, no survivors, no interested friends. The woman lived in Madison but not a single one of her neighbors knew her."

"What kind of an accident was it?"

"Well, it totaled the car. She hit an abutment and cartwheeled off an overpass and fell twenty-five feet."

Roger was on the extension, having overcome his unease at the thought of contact with Verda Graham.

"Where's the car now?"

"Who's that?"

"Roger," Philip explained.

"You want to buy it?"

"Was it checked for fingerprints?"

"Fingerprints! What in the world for?"

"Then it wasn't?"

The car had been checked for fingerprints when it was found abandoned in Baraboo a few weeks before, but that had been in a forlorn effort to track down the thief. A totaled automobile in a single-vehicle accident was another thing entirely.

Roger became obsessed with the idea that the fatal car should have been examined carefully, but it was difficult to know what prompted his obsession. Did he think evidence of foul play would be found? Roger only shrugged.

"I don't know why. Except that a husband committing suicide and his widow dying in an accident weeks later teases the mind."

Not the mind of Verda Graham, as it happened. She was not at all disposed to satisfy Roger's inexplicable curiosity.

"Roger, be reasonable. She would do me a favor if it made any sense. This request makes no sense."

"Let's go back to Wisconsin."

"What for?"

Another item in the *Village Ear* concerned the search for someone to take the place of the late Albert Clinton. Philip called Felicia Webster Leamon and learned that the new curator was Bernard Skye. Roger said he would make a few calls and half an hour later Philip found him seated immobile at his computer, the screen dead, staring into space.

"No luck?"

"Skye has had a checkered career."

"A cabbie?"

"He was fired from one paleography job under suspicion of conspiring to steal some priceless materials."

"It's a little late to tell Felicia that."

"She should have been told."

"Well, obviously she wasn't."

*   *   *

For two days Roger was preoccupied, his troubled silence more unnervingly nagging than a voiced reproach could ever be. Philip felt that there was something he should be doing that he was not doing, but he was not at all sure what it was. Was Roger pained because Philip had not importuned Verda Graham, cajoled her into having the wreck in which Jane Clinton had died given the full treatment? Did he simply miss the idyllic solitude of Wisconsin and the proximity of all the papers and effects of a poet he admired? Whatever, the solution to the problem seemed to present itself when Philip received an enigmatic call from Felicia's husband Frank.

"Some letters Felicia kept in the attic are missing."

"A break-in?"

He hesitated. "Actually, I took them. Look, the foundation my wife set up has problems."

Fifteen minutes later, it was unclear why exactly Frank had called. Philip would not have worked for the man if he had asked. But he wasn't asked, and that made the call more difficult to forget. And then he received a report from his Frequent Flyer plan.

"We can leave for Madison tomorrow," he told Roger.

"Really!" But he repressed his joy. "Another case?"

"Same one."

"Felicia called?"

Finally he told Roger how they were going and three hundred pounds of genius turned crestfallen. "Philip, you couldn't justify the expense."

"I'm flying free and I can upgrade us both so you can have a seat you'll fit into."

They packed and drove to LaGuardia the following morning. Two and a half hours later then descended into Billy Mitchell Field in clear sunny weather, picked up their rental van and drove into Milwaukee. Off the road, gaudily advertised, were several low structures featuring adult videos and books.

"No children's?" Roger asked.

He was serious. Philip started to explain, then stopped. How amazing that a man as talented and knowledgeable as Roger should yet be so naive. But what was to be gained from telling a bibliophile that adult books were aimed at the morally stunted?

"I'll let Felicia know I'm here," Philip said, changing the subject. "Professional courtesy."

"We should speak to Aran as well."

"Aran!"

"Howard Webster's last wife."

"I know who she is. Why should we speak to her?"

"I want to ask her something about some allusions in *The Leaden Echo*."

2

MRS. LEAMON had okayed the purchase of a CD player and Bernard Skye was tilted back in the chair in the study in which Howard Webster had read and napped, eyes closed, a beatific smile on his face as the strains of Mozart filled the room. Skye's appreciation of music was more animal than rational, a response to the ordered sound that insinuated itself into his emotions and bore him along, suggesting that life made sense, that ideas were the corruption of feeling, that all was right with the world.

And so in a sense it was. Ober, hired on his own authority by Skye, had been a godsend. What in a better day would have been called a jewel. Skye opened his eyes, turned in his chair and looked out back where Ober was even now methodically chopping firewood.

Funny guy. Hard to imagine what Webster had seen in him, letting him hang around the place during his last days. And now he was back.

"Didn't you know he was dead?"

Ober nodded. "Someone told me he wrote a story and I was in it."

"That's right."

"You read it?"

He had read it since running into Ober in the village. Would he have thought it a great story if it didn't have Howard Webster's name on it? Maybe. But it was Webster's authorship that explained the sales of the slender volume, the first prose fiction by the poet, a work that survived its author and that might have gone undiscovered for who knows how long if it hadn't been for Clinton. Skye had no thoughts about his predecessor, except that the guy had kept busy as a bee. Gotten a lot of work done in the time he was here, loading up the computer. And Skye's first task had been to unload it. Now that he had figured out what Felicia was up to he was putting his mind to ways in which he could turn it to his advantage. That black mark of the Princeton job had been, he now saw, a positive credential as far as Howard Webster's daughter was concerned. She was walking off with holographs and manuscripts right and left, and she didn't want records of their having belonged to the foundation. The assumption was that Bernard Skye would not notice or if he did that he would not blow the whistle. What moral authority did he have to accuse someone else of manuscript theft—if the daughter of the poet could be said to be stealing something that had been part of her inheritance from her father?

"The hi-fi system here is ancient," he had remarked earlier that week.

She had turned from the file cabinet.

"What we need is a good CD player." He kept his eyes on the manuscript she had taken from the cabinet.

"I suppose it does get lonely here."

"I'll order one, okay?"

No need to say it, it was a little bargain driven on the basis of his finally understanding the point of her visits to the farm to load up her briefcase.

It was not lost on Ober, however.

"She's taking things away? Why?"

Ober looked at Skye over the rim of his glass. Evening,
the sun over the yardarm or its rural Wisconsin equivalent
and they were out on the porch, drinking.

"Souvenirs of her old man's work."

"I got the impression they weren't close."

"He left her everything."

But what was everything? The records Clinton had so carefully made were now lost in the electronic bowels of the
computer, perhaps recoverable by some arcane means—Skye
had been told that nothing is ever irretrievably lost, well
almost nothing, even when it has been erased from the
disk—but for all practical purposes there was no list to which
the papers, manuscripts and letters could be put in one-to-
one correspondence. That is why Felicia could walk away
with briefcases filled with her father's literary remains. That
is why anyone else could do the same. Except that Skye's
backup of the data he had erased from the hard disk was in
a safe-deposit box in the village, a little insurance.

With Clinton's record gone from the computer anyone
could walk off with unregistered material. If the thought
occurred to him it must have occurred to his employer as
well, so what had she done to safeguard against it? Perhaps
nothing, but he could not afford to assume that. And a good
thing too. The realization had come with an inevitability
that put it beyond doubt. Who guarded the guardian of the
papers of the Howard Webster Foundation? Ober.

Skye despite himself smiled at the realization. Having the
old fart around was more interesting when he realized that
Ober was keeping an eye on him.

That this wasn't just his imagination became clear in the
days that followed. Ober would suddenly appear in the
house, standing in the library door if Skye was in the study
or silently entering the kitchen when Skye was in the library,
so that he would feel those rheumy old eyes on him, look
up and there he was.

"How's it going, Ober?"

A shrug. Ober liked to work outside, or said he did. He had fixed up a place in the barn, a chair, an old gooseneck lamp, a place to read. It was what had surprised Webster in the man he took to be a tramp. Ober was a very literate man. So maybe he spent more time reading than working around the place, but who cared. Not Skye. He might think he had hired Ober but the old man's surveillance disabused him of that notion. The sense of being watched was welcome, oddly enough. It was good to know, good to realize that, whatever he decided to do, he would have to be careful to make it undetectable by Ober and Felicia. If he could do that, he was home free, because who else was there? Clinton was dead and now so was his widow, though she probably hadn't known anything anyway.

Maybe the single most valuable item in the collection was the manuscript of *The Leaden Echo*, but that was too widely and generally known to be a tempting target.

"Want to see the story he wrote about you?" he asked Ober.

He opened the plastic folder in which it was kept and extended it to Ober so that he could remove the manuscript. The old man leafed through the manuscript while Skye looked on benevolently.

"He must have been writing that during the days you were here with him."

"You think so?"

"He had to. When exactly did you leave?"

"That was a long time ago. Why?"

"I wonder how many days intervened between your departure and his suicide."

"When he might have been writing this?"

"Webster was alive when you left the farm, wasn't he, Ober?"

The old man looked at him. If the question bothered him, he gave no sign. "As alive as I am now."

Skye held out the plastic container and had Ober slip the manuscript in. Done. The manuscript was now negotiable. Skye himself had never handled the manuscript, but now it had Ober's prints on it.

3

IT WAS fortunate that Roger was delighted to be back in Wisconsin because Felicia Leamon certainly showed no pleasure at seeing him again.

"I mailed a check," she said, puzzled. Did she think Philip had come personally to collect his bill?

"I received it. Thank you. But I can't convince myself I did what I was hired to do."

"Oh, but you did. The manuscript is back."

"True, but no thanks to me. Besides, the circumstances of its . . ."

"Mr. Knight, I appreciate your conscientiousness, but I can only wish you had telephoned me before returning. I assure you I am satisfied with what you've already done. I do not wish to employ your services further."

That was definite enough, too definite. Philip decided not to mention the call he had received from her husband. He left her and walked back to the hotel where Roger awaited, eager to continue on to the Webster Library.

"We won't be going, Roger."

"Why?"

He gave a brief and blunt account of his talk with Felicia.

"You mean we won't go as her employees. But the library is open to those interested in the work of Howard Webster."

It stung Philip to be sent packing. On the other hand, it would be unprofessional to continue as if he were still in Felicia's employ. Who knows what he would have done if a call to his answering service hadn't told him Verda Graham was trying to reach him?

"I'm in Milwaukee," he said, when he got through to her.

"I hope you didn't come all this way in anticipation of important results from an examination of the car?"

"Verda, I understand. It was only a hope . . ."

"Oh, I managed to get it done. But it was a waste of time. The only fresh prints other than Mrs. Clinton's are those found in it when it was recovered in Baraboo."

"Fresh prints?"

Verda cleared her throat. "Fresh since the car was recovered. We have a division of opinion in the lab. Our view is that they must date from the time the car was stolen."

"Why?"

"Because any other interpretation is irrelevant. She was alone in the car."

"What time did the accident occur?" Roger asked, having picked up the extension in the bathroom.

"Who's that?"

"My brother Roger."

"Is he in Milwaukee too?"

"He wanted to visit the Webster Library again in any case."

"What time did the accident occur?" Roger asked.

"The wreck was found in the morning. Five in the morning."

"So it happened during the night?"

"Yes."

"With no witnesses?"

"With no witnesses."

Philip smiled. Roger's question had a way of making one feel vaguely delinquent, as if something that obviously should have been done had been overlooked.

"How long are you going to be in Wisconsin, Phil?"

"Maybe I'll come on down to Madison while my brother is doing research at the farm."

"I can show you around."

"Good."

"The WBI," she added, but her voice sounded uncharacteristically sultry.

After he hung up, the bathroom door opened and Roger shuffled into the room. "I don't have to go out to the Webster Library."

"Nonsense. After coming all this way? Of course we'll go there."

Verda, while tall, was well-proportioned and graceful and her blue unblinking eyes had a disturbing yet easeful effect on him. He got away from Roger seldom enough nowadays and while he did not resent the time his helpless brother required—the duty to look after Roger had more than once saved him from entangling alliances—a man had to have a chance to look up old friends once in a while. Meanwhile, he promised Roger he would get in touch with Aran.

"Maybe she still wants to hire you."

"For what?"

"What did she want before?"

"The moon."

Whatever she wanted, it was a lawyer she needed, not a detective. If there was a legal way of prying any of the wealth lately realized from Howard Webster's work away from the foundation his daughter had created, it would doubtless consume much time and money, however, and Aran had been unwilling to wait. She had not in so many words asked if he would steal for her, but that is what it came down to. Philip had no intention of jeopardizing his reputation or his licence, but speaking with the great poet's third wife seemed a small price to pay for a side trip to Madison.

4

"YOU'RE AS beautiful as ever, Aran."

As if everything was just as it had been when they were living together on the farm. Who would believe that within minutes of being reunited with a man thought to be dead she would be scolding him for the way he had treated her? And complaining that she had been prevented from sharing in his belated success. And she told him of Felicia's bitch-in-the-manger management of his royalties.

"She's not as disinterested as you think."

"Well, she tied it all up in that damnable foundation."

"I'm pleased about that."

"Where have you been for two years?"

"That's a long story."

"Write it down. You'll make another fortune."

He shook his head, the smile the same but his eyes more thoughtful than she remembered them. "I'm dead and I'm going to stay dead."

"But you have to live. Howard, all that money is yours! How can others inherit it if you're still alive?"

"Have you any idea how pleasant it is to have survived myself and seen what critics say of the late Howard Webster? I'll be frank with you, Aran. I'm surprised. After you left me . . ."

"Left you!"

"With cause, my dear. I grant you that. I was a devil to live with, I can see that now. Alone, I could not fight the thought that my life, my career, everything, amounted to nothing. Since I was a young man I sacrificed everything to the notion that I was meant to be a great poet. The results were in and what was the verdict? Did anyone remember Howard Webster, going to pot on his farm in Wisconsin?"

"All you would have had to do is publish that novel yourself."

This suggestion did not please him. He was a poet primarily and did not wish to be praised for prose fiction.

"Howard, all your poetry is in print again."

He told her about Sardinia and Sant'Antioco, about the months of loneliness he had spent in purgatory.

"I had died and gone to Dante and he guided me through an island he'd never seen in life, preparing me, though I didn't know it. Aran, I came near despair on the farm, but I never really doubted my talent and my achievement. In Sardinia I had time to reflect on what I had done. No one could ever convince me that my work did not deserve acclaim."

He spoke matter-of-factly, without the old braggadocio and vanity. And then one day, when his soul had been readied for it, he sat down in a barber shop and picked up a magazine that told him what had happened in his absence.

"I had been dead but now I was alive again."

And as soon as he returned to the country he looked her up. Aran, having had the satisfaction of berating Howard, the sonofabitch, sat back and smiled receptively as he told her what it had been like to be dead and not know anything that was happening in the States and then, suddenly, out of the blue, picking up an old magazine and reading about himself. The drink she made for him stood more or less ignored on the table beside his chair. That more than anything else convinced Aran that this was not the old Howard.

"So what are you going to do?"

He held out his hand and she rose and went to him. That he should stay with her went without saying. They had all the time in the world to decide what Howard would do next.

"Not on your life," he said the next morning when she asked if he meant to make a big announcement. Of course she was thinking of what a scoop it would be.

"How then?"

"Aran," he said softly, covering her hand and leaning toward her, "I don't intend to come back. That would spoil everything."

She thought he was kidding. If he wanted to stay dead he should have remained in Sardinia.

1
PART FOUR

DID IT matter that Bernard Skye had witnessed her systematic looting of the file cabinets at the farm? He would have to be blind not to notice, but then she had hired him because of his background. A man whose professional integrity, or alleged lack of it, had put him out of work was not an accuser she need fear. At least that had been her theory. And as Skye settled in at the farm, dutifully following her irrational instructions that he destroy the careful records Clinton had embarked on, thus turning everything into unrecorded, hence unknown, material, she carried off what appeared to her to be the cream of the crop. More than once she'd almost overcome her reluctance and carried off the manuscript of the novella that had propelled her father into posthumous glory. But that would have been pure folly. It could never be numbered among the papers it was her plan to announce she had refrained from donating to the Webster Foundation and would put on the market because of sudden and unforeseen financial need.

"That sonofabitch Hector," Frank muttered, as weeks passed and there was no word from the man he had allowed to act as his agent in selling the letters he had stolen from the attic. Frank pulled at his lower lip as he glowered into space, a bad habit recently acquired. Would his lip loosen and hang slack, revealing his long lower teeth? Why is it always the lower teeth men show? Felicia found herself pulling at her own upper lip.

"Stop doing that," she said to Frank.

He was genuinely surprised. "What?"

She showed him. He took his fingers from his mouth and stared at them as if they belonged to someone else. He might have been addressing them when he said, "We'll never see any of that money."

"Forget those letters, forget Hector, write them off as a loss."

"Felicia, I have explained how much money I've lost."

"Write it all off."

"I am not making out my taxes, I am talking about honest-to-God severe money problems."

"I am preparing a solution."

His lower lip snapped into place. His wary eyes softened into hope. "The other letters?"

"Better than that."

She told him of her systematic sacking of the farmhouse files. They went upstairs to the spare bedroom where she unlocked the closet and showed him what she had gathered.

"Repossessed. They were mine and they are mine."

"My God." His eyes shone with greed. Had it been a mistake to show him this treasure?

"If you so much as touch one sheet of these . . ."

He lifted his hand and with closed eyes shook his head. "As God is my judge, Felicia. But what's your plan?"

He made whiskey sours and they sat up until one in the morning chattering together as they hadn't in years and when they went upstairs she allowed him into her bed but he was so distracted by the thought of all the money they were going to get from her father's papers that he was useless. He held her tightly, his ineffectual limpness pressed warmly against her thigh, and it was tender if nothing else. Had she been recovering those papers all along as an offering to Frank? The thought would have repelled her hours before but now, snug in her husband's arms, it was difficult to say where she left off and he began.

"Where are you taking all those papers?"

Felicia, leaning over an open file drawer, involuntarily lurched at Skye's question but she did not turn.

"I want some of these things at home."

"In Milwaukee?"

She turned. "What are you working on this morning?"

Rain ran down the window behind him. He leaned against the radiator for its warmth, bundled in a bulky white knit sweater, his loafered feet crossed. His whole posture was insolent.

"The usual."

"And what is that?"

"Breathing out and breathing in. What I was hired to do."

"Are you becoming bored with the job?"

"The job?" He smiled. "We both know why I was hired."

Felicia pushed the file drawer shut with her hip and turned to him. "We both know this is the only job you are likely to get."

He pushed away from the radiator, his face flushed. Anger? Shame?

"Have you finished cataloguing the books?"

"It's a big job."

"You can alternate it with yard work, so you don't atrophy. Your predecessor went mad, probably too much time spent indoors."

"Ober does the yard work."

Felicia avoided Ober, wondering why Skye accepted the man's claim to be the model for the tramp in *The Leaden Echo*. Anyone who'd read it could have come up the drive and claimed to be Ober, but why would anyone want to? Felicia had preferred skepticism about the man to learning that he actually had stayed here with her father during his last days.

"I don't want him to stay here."

"Fire him."

"I never hired him."

"All he gets is room and board anyway."

"Tell him he must go."

Skye shook his head. "Uh uh. Talk to him, you'll see why I'm reluctant."

"But that's ridiculous. He has no right to remain here."

"Tell him that."

She spent the afternoon trying to catch a glimpse of Ober but the man knew enough to get in out of the rain. Skye told her Ober had made a nest for himself in the barn.

"He's no trouble out there."

How could he stand being out there where Clinton had hanged himself?

About three-thirty she took her briefcase and, propping the porch door open before opening her umbrella, called to Skye that she was leaving. No answer. He was still down for his afternoon nap. Well, why not? She ran out to her car and pulled open the driver's door, getting ready for the moment of exposure when she shut up her umbrella and ducked into the car. And then she saw Ober standing under the eave of the barn, his beret pulled low over his eyes, puffing on a cigarette. For a spooky moment he looked like someone else. No wonder her father had written of him as if he were his other self.

She closed her umbrella and ducked into the car, pulling

the door closed after her. Before starting the motor, she turned and looked through windows running with rain at the lonely figure standing under the eave of the barn and felt a tender sadness she had not felt since she was a girl.

2

"YOU'RE NOT dead, so all that money is yours," Aran urged.

"I'm touched by your concern."

"Howard, you're out of money. What will you live on?"

"My farm. I get room and board. What more does a man need?"

"Fame? Glory?"

"Precisely why I must remain dead. Have you any idea what my resurrection would do to the interest in my work?"

"Sure. Double it, triple it, more."

He doubted it. In fact, he was certain she was wrong. Reading the tributes that Bullitt and Shea and Garcia had written, Webster noted the valedictory tone. Praise for a dead competitor came easily, it was in its way a manner of drawing attention to oneself, the Bullitt tribute to Webster, what Garcia and Shea said of the man whose late work they had savaged in reviews. They were capable of magnanimity now. Why envy a success that Howard Webster could not enjoy? And of course they would find in his posthumous triumph a basis for hoping that their own careers might be resuscitated. If he came back to life and walked among them again, their belated affection would turn to hate. Of course they would all see it as a consummate scheme, taking the Salinger ploy to its apotheosis. They would turn on him like ravening beasts, all the flaws in his work would suddenly become clear, the novella would be recognized as overrated.

The novella. How it rankled that the story Clinton had based on the notebook he'd kept of the weeks Ober was with him should have been the basis for his late success. Hitherto his notebook had been only daily jottings, the habit of a lifetime, thoughts that might perhaps turn into poems if the muse should visit him again. Clinton, may he rot in hell, had transformed the account of those days with Ober into a story Webster could not bring himself to hate. It was well-written, well-told, a haunting memoir, evoking thoughts of *Ethan Frome, Death in Venice, Kreutzer Sonata.* Who would have expected such power from that wimp of a curator? If he despised the novella, thought of it as junk, he could have tolerated its being the improbable means whereby his own work had come to be appreciated. But it was a good novella and critic after critic had lamented the fact that Howard Webster had not discovered his true gift earlier. The poetry was competent, from time to time it veered toward greatness, but it was read as the verse of the author of *The Leaden Echo.* Whether he liked it or not, his reputation was inextricably entwined with what Clinton had done, indeed was a pendant on the curator's accomplishment.

Now he knew what he must do to earn his newfound reputation.

He must get to work writing again. He must produce writings of Howard Webster that Aran could announce to the world, things he had left to her, mailed her in his last days. She could say she had stored the package, assuming it contained personal things of hers he wanted to rid the house of.

The drama would be Howard Webster's realization in his last days that his love for Aran survived. Thus it would be as the grieving widow that she would offer to the world these newly found writings of her late husband, Howard Webster.

Aran wept when he told her his plan. She came into his arms, choosing to think of what he had said as a simple confession of love rather than as a scheme to cash in on his posthumous reputation. It was a tender moment during which Webster himself was tempted by insincerity. But if there had been anything of which he had become convinced during his sojourn in Sardinia it was that all his wives were mistakes. Felicia's mother Vivian, Helen, God rest their souls. And Aran most of all. He could see what had attracted him to her. The high cheekbones, the chaste planes of her face, the sculpted head he could enclose in both his hands, the agile eager body. Making love with her stirred remembered ashes into flame but after desire was spent, holding her in his arms, he knew that that was all there had ever been between them, what was now clinically called an exchange of bodily fluids. God what an age! Reading newspapers, listening to television, he found himself half thankful he was dead.

The great difficulty with his plan was that when he sat down to write nothing happened. It was an impotence far worse than that he had felt in Sardinia, when for over a year he had been free of desire for a woman. That had been at once liberating and sad, as if he had indeed died. But even in those dark days he had nursed the conviction that he would at some time sit down and compose again. He was husbanding his strength, allowing his imagination to store up images, letting them live in his unconscious; sooner or later they would come forth and he would write them down, taking dictation from his daimon. But seated at his makeshift desk in the barn, ready at last, the page before him stared blankly back at him.

After two days of that, he tried priming the pump by writing out poems he had written years ago. It might have worked if he had not been reminded of the long hours spent copying out *The Leaden Echo* with Clinton lying in a diabetic coma in the library. That exercise had not been a chore, he had kept at it in a state of exhilaration, conscious that he was copying out something of exceptional value. He did not get this sense as he made copies of long-ago poems, even of those he would have thought his best. The depressing realization descended upon him that he was second rate, doomed to be forgotten, a few copies of his books surviving to show up in garage sales or library bargains when the shelves were cleared. The handful of anthologized poems would eventually disappear. How many poets of the forties and fifties were still anthologized? Leafing through successive editions of Oscar Williams's *Golden Treasury* was a lesson in literary mortality, the brief moment in the sun enjoyed by the minor poet and then the waters closed over and that was that. His own fate had been sealed before his unlooked-for death but the revival inescapably was tied to the book Clinton had written. Whatever fame and glory were his were phony, based on a mistake, stolen.

He tore up the page on which he had been writing and stared gloomily across the barn. There was the beam from which Ober had hanged himself and on which he had strung up the lifeless body of Albert Clinton. A notebook, a diary, that is what he must do. A notebook had been the origin of *The Leaden Echo*.

The doors of the barn swung open as if to shout in silent horror. Webster moved back with the opening doors, then stood staring into the barn where a shaft of admitted sun ignited Ober's body. He crossed himself without thinking, the instinctive act of a believing peasant, which is what he longed to be. Now in the presence of death, prayer or at least talking to himself came easily. He edged closer to the hanging body, son semblable, son frère. Ober was horribly dead, the rope having choked life and color and comeliness from his face. The swollen tongue emerged, purplish from purple lips, ugly. Webster began to gag, but it was just the dry heaves, fair enough, he had been drunk when he opened the doors but he was sober now. As instinctively as he had crossed himself he cut down the body, turning away from its sickening collapse upon the dusty floor of the barn.

Reader, it is here the story is amended . . . the thought crowding the poet's mind was that he himself lay dead, that some surrogate of himself had been hung by the neck until dead and that he was no longer real. Near-death experiences had always fascinated him, as once the book by Aldous Huxley's widow had. How infinitely more attractive than the other world of Dante, the notion that each of us steps at death into light, this world and its deeds, dark or otherwise, an irrelevancy . . . all souls are equal in that bourn from which no traveler returns. That had been Huxley, that was the common note of near-death experiences. An inexpressible joy as the soul strained toward a light, freeing itself from the body.

Bury the dead, comfort the sorrowful. It was a comfort to Webster to set about disposing of the mortal remains of his alter ego. The obvious course would be to telephone the village but even to think that was to reject it. Another thought took precedence. By cremating the body of Ober I will fashion my own departure from the world.

How stale flat pale and unprofitable seemed to me all the uses of this world . . . here I was an old poet on a barren farm who had spent weeks drinking and quarreling with an oddly literate tramp who in some mystical

*way was myself. I would not deliver him over to the
village undertaker. The task of disposing of his remains
was mine and I welcomed it. Dear God, the adrenaline
that pumped through me as I gathered wood for the
pyre. I wheeled the body out to it in a barrow and
heaved him up on the dry kindling. Even so I soaked
the pyre with gasoline, bothered by images of Adolf's
inner circle disposing of him and Eva in the yard outside
the bunker while the Russians bore down on that ulti-
mate redoubt, götterdämmerung indeed.*

*Once the fire was lit I walked away in the clothes I
wore, reconciled to being the late Howard Webster . . .*

He had found his line at last, his pen moved rapidly over
the page. Eventually he longed to sit down again with his
notebook and recount the year and a half he had spent
unware of what had occurred in the wake of his supposed
death.

3

"THINK OF it as a vacation," Roger had advised.

"In Milwaukee!"

"What's wrong with Milwaukee?"

There didn't have to be anything wrong with it for Milwaukee to rank low on his list of places he would go to relax. The truth was he felt like an ambulance chaser, coming back here on his own. And being rebuffed by Felicia Leamon made it much worse. Any self-respecting PI would have shaken the dust of the place from his sandals and headed back to Rye. The call from her husband had been enigmatic in the extreme, he refused to say just what new business the Webster Foundation might wish Philip Knight to pursue. Nor was Aran the third wife any more promising. He should drive all thoughts of Wisconsin from his head. But that was to reckon without Roger.

In the morning news there had been an item on letters of Howard Webster which had appeared in a dealer's catalogue in New Jersey.

"That's Holly," Roger cried. "B. G. Hollander. He lives in Princeton."

"It looks like Felicia is finally cashing in on her father's popularity."

If that was it she was operating through intermediaries. Roger called Holly and Philip suffered through the long-distance exchange of greetings, Roger like a bumptious boy. Apparently the art dealer in Princeton was responding in kind. Philip gave up. Sober and serious citizens turned out to be nerds and Roger and his friends, geniuses all, acted like schoolboys. Phil went into the bathroom, shut the door and glared at himself in the mirror. Who was he to decide what outer should match what inner?

"He has over a dozen Webster letters," Roger reported. "Webster letters to his first wife, very rare."

"Where did he get them?"

"Dealers never tell."

"Maybe they were stolen."

Roger shook his head, making his jowls quiver, then his belly, then assorted blubber all over his body. "One thing is certain. Holly would never deal in stolen goods."

"Then it has to be Felicia."

"He says no."

"I thought dealers never talked."

"Like Socrates's daimon, they give negative answers only."

"Hmmm." It was best to let such obscurities ride. Asking what they meant was fatal, inevitably calling forth an explanation more confusing than the original remark. *Obscurum per obscurius.* He had the phrase from Roger. It meant what it sounded like.

"She seems the likely source, needless to say."

"Or her husband."

He had not told Roger the story of Frank Leamon. It was the kind of thing one learned on the edges of any investigation, information of no relevance to the case, but coming willy-nilly. It had been Frank's secretary who had, unwittingly, given a hint which when pursued turned up the facts. How take a phone call from such a man seriously? Philip had met his like before but there was something magnificent in the frequency and drama of Frank's business failures. The entrepreneurial spirit, Philip had come to think, is more spiritual than materialistic, far more altruistic than greedy, in the sense that Frank was in it for the game, the risk, the excitement, not the money. Money had never come his way, of course, but if it had he would quickly have gotten rid of it in order to begin again the pursuit of the dream. Such irrational optimism did not exclude larceny of course but Philip felt he knew how Frank had come into possession of those letters. How could they be stolen if Felicia had given them to her husband?

Those letters, tantalizingly described by Holly on the phone, only whetted Roger's desire to get back to the farm where he could wallow in Howard Webster papers.

"I have no client."

"We'll go as scholars."

"No."

Roger saw how awkward it was for Philip.

"Get in touch with Aran, the third wife. She was dying to hire you a few weeks ago."

Aran. The image of her eyes, the birdlike movements of her head, the anguish in her voice as she begged him to become her investigator as well as Felicia's. Had she ever really understood what a conflict of interest that would have been? Roger's suggestion made sense, and the letters in the morning news provided an opening gambit.

"What letters?" Aran asked, when he telephoned her. She had sounded unsure who he was.

"I'd rather tell you in person."

"But why do you think they concern me?"

"Your husband's letters?"

"I am sick and tired of Howard Webster," she cried. "I want to be left alone and forget him . . ."

"Are you free for lunch?"

"You aren't listening to me at all."

"I'll come by the *Journal* at noon."

But the phone had already gone dead.

At the *Journal* he walked past the receptionist and headed for the elevators. As with hospitals, the trick was to look as if you knew where you were going and get past the guardians of the inner sancta. Once on the elevator or on any floor above, asking directions was safer. But as he neared the elevators, he saw the great expanse of the newsroom just ahead and continued on to there.

"Where's Aran Webster?" he asked as he came to the first desk.

A phone was lifted and passed to him, by a man whose eyes did not leave the screen of his word processor. "Extension 495."

"Just dial it?"

"Yeah."

He dialed 495 and as he waited for it to be answered he saw Aran on the far side of the room, holding a paper cup of coffee and talking with a man and a woman. She glanced at her phone, but made no move to answer it. Philip let it ring until finally, with an air of exasperation, she picked it up.

"Sorry to interrupt. This is Philip Knight."

Is this what it would be like with televised phoning? She frowned at the mention of his name and looked at the ceiling as if seeking help there. Then she remembered. But pleasure at the memory was fleeting. The frown was back when she asked him what he wanted.

"I hoped we could get together."

"Why should I talk with a detective working for the woman who robbed me of my inheritance?"

"I am currently unemployed."

"Is that right?"

"Yes. When can I see you?"

"What's the point?"

"I want to ask you some questions about Howard Webster."

"No!"

She shut her eyes and shook her head as she said it, then she repeated it. He was able to remove the phone from his ear before she slammed hers down. He thanked the man for the use of his phone, got a nod, and looked up to see Aran bearing down on him although she had not seen him. Philip turned away and let her go past. No need to start a scene.

She went past the elevators and into the reception area where she used a public pay phone. Odd, when she had a phone on her desk. Philip out of a generic curiosity managed to get close enough to hear her speak.

"Howard? I have to see you."

Howard? Philip kept his mind a blank as he followed her from the building and then followed her car through the streets of Milwaukee to where she lived.

He felt slightly sleazy and fraudulent. What had become of him, pursuing business like this? The whole point of moving to Rye and getting the 800 number was to work on his own terms, to take no job that didn't appeal to him. He had become used to potential clients begging him to accept a job, he had become practiced in turning them down. And here he was in Milwaukee forcing himself on a poor working woman who had every right to her privacy.

In counterpoint to this self-criticism was the memory of her on the phone. "Howard? I have to see you."

He put glasses on her apartment windows and soon was rewarded by a glimpse of Aran. The PI as voyeur. His was not a dignified profession. He wondered if Roger realized that, or if he cared. And then he saw the man.

A familiar man. Why? He had had just a glimpse and he kept the glasses on the apartment, waiting for more . . .

There was a metallic tapping on the passenger window. A patrolman bent to look in at him, brows raised.

"What are you doing?"

"I'm on surveillance."

The officer shook his head. "I checked out the car."

"I'm a private investigator."

"Sure you are. Sam Voyeur."

"That's pretty good." He reached for his billfold and the officer stepped back warily. Philip displayed his licence and the officer came squinting back.

"That's a New York licence."

"Wisconsin and New York recognize one another's licencing."

"Who you looking at?"

"A client."

"Someone phoned in and said a strange man was looking at people through binoculars."

"Now you know."

"How long you going to be here?"

"That's hard to say."

It was two hours later that Aran came out of the building, alone, or so it seemed at first. She walked to the curb, looked up and down and then turned. The man joined her. And then Philip knew who he must be.

Ober. The tramp who had returned to Howard Webster's farm, the man who had spent the poet's last days with him.

4

IN THE weeks that followed Felicia's huffiness about Ober, the itinerant was an infrequent presence. Several times, Skye had concluded that Ober had gone for good but then he would show up again, hole up in the barn and be worthless so far as company went. The solitude was beginning to tell on Skye, no doubt of that. He had taken to leaving the television on in the living room even when he was listening to music in the study. It gave the illusion that he was not alone in the house. Unfortunately he had no stomach for daytime television fare and the loneliness was far from enabling him to overcome his reluctance to actually watch such bilge. But the murmuring set established that beyond the confines of this Wisconsin farm there was a great world where people in numbers jostled and shoved and competed with one another. And worried about getting mugged. Here Skye was more likely to be attacked by wild beasts than a fellow human being. In short, the isolation and freedom which at first had been so powerfully attractive now grated on him. The thought of a scheduled day with a taskmaster seeing that he stuck to his last exerted an almost sensuous attraction. Here he could spend his day any way he wanted. So much freedom canceled itself out. He seemed condemned to live randomly.

He spent more and more time asleep, retiring at ten and staying buried under comforters and an electric blanket until nine the following morning. The more sleep he got the more tired he became. He added an afternoon nap to the mix, dozing off for two hours and more. If he could get his sleeping time up to twenty-four hours a day life would be tolerable. No wonder he was pissed at Ober for preferring the barn to the house when he was on the premises, seemingly eager to pull those big double doors closed behind him. Skye tried to see what the guy was doing out there, but no window gave him a good view. He found a board in which a knothole was rotting out and he helped it along, gouging out a peeping hole. Ober had made a kind of desk of the workbench and he was pulled up to it, bent over, writing diligently. Skye watched him long enough to see that this wasn't the activity of a moment. Ober had the look of a man settled down to a prolonged task, and for the fifteen or twenty minutes Skye peered in at him, Ober went on writing. After his nap, Skye went again to his peephole. Ober was still writing.

Such diligence shamed him, but it puzzled him even more. What would that old tramp have to write that took so long? This curiosity grew but he sensed it would do no good to question Ober directly about it. Instead Skye developed the theory that the tramp had been moved to imitate the great man he had lived with during his last hours. Maybe writing seemed something anyone might do, simply a matter of sitting down and doing it. Well, it was at least that, and there was Ober sitting down and putting his hand to it. Oblique efforts to get him talking about Webster's work, as a prelude to prying into what he was writing out in the barn, failed to work. Skye grew uncomfortable with the thought that a dissolute tramp could by sheer willpower do what Skye himself had never done.

Of course Skye believed that, if he tried, he would succeed as a writer. He had been a consumer of fiction all his life and it was easy to imagine that he could produce the sort of thing he admired. Complete, on the page, ready to be enjoyed, finished poetry or fiction seemed so inevitable it was difficult to imagine a process in which things might have developed wholly differently than they actually had in the finished work. Skye had written down lines that occurred to him, one or two at a time, seldom more, and these seemed installments against the day when he would at last effortlessly produce great works of imagination. Surprise at what Ober was doing altered to uneasiness and then became pique and finally jealousy. He had to know what Ober was up to.

"Can you drive, Ober?"

"Why?"

"I wondered if you'd run an errand for me in the village."

"Not now."

"Why not?"

An evasive look. How could he say that he had to get back to his writing without making it a topic of conversation? There seemed little doubt that writing was a secret process for Ober. Skye took some comfort in the thought that this meant the man had no confidence in what he was writing.

"What do you need?"

He made up a long list for the supermarket and for the liquor store and asked Ober to stop by the pharmacy too. As soon as Ober reached the road and turned the car toward the village Skye ran out to the barn, grabbed the door handle and pulled. Pain flared in the socket of his arm when the door did not give. It was locked! Skye was furious. Who did that sonofabitch think he was, locking the barn? Skye had not noticed before that the door could be locked. He kicked the door and then circled the building. In the back, high above, a door opening into the loft hung open. A ladder. But the only ladder he could remember having seen was in the barn. He looked despairingly up at that possible entree to the loft. Finally he trudged angrily back to the house where on the porch his mood changed completely when he noticed the stepladder, folded, leaning against the wall of the house. He snatched it up and ran out behind the barn where he opened it and began to climb, slowly. Heights had always bothered him, but he didn't even think of that as he mounted the ladder, steadying himself by pressing his hands against the wall of the barn. He got to the very top and stood there, pressed tightly against the barn and slowly raised his eyes. The bottom of the loft door was just inches above his head.

The task now was to lever himself up and into the loft. He made the mistake of looking down and the precariousness of his perch made him begin to tremble, causing the ladder to shake and increasing his peril. Impulsively he reached up, opened the loft door wider and saw a metal ring embedded in the inside frame of the door. He grasped that, angled himself off the top of the ladder and lifted one leg until his shoe slid onto the floor of the loft. Pulling on the ring, he began to lift himself but as he did, the door closed, clamping onto his ankle. Below him the stepladder teetered and fell. Panic filled him. He could not get down the way he had come, and he was dangling against the side of the barn, two hands and a foot wedged under a door which wanted to close. He actually yelped in desperation.

But then he got his free foot against the barn, pushed outward, opening the door, and lifted himself sufficiently to see the dark, warm loft inviting him like the womb. He managed to throw his body upward and inward, his hip caught on the floor of the loft, and he rolled into the darkness. He lay on his back, sobbing with relief, looking up to where what seemed to be an owl perched motionless on a roof support. A different fear passed over him as he scrambled to his feet and ran huddled over to the edge of the loft.

Below and to the right was the workbench. Whatever Ober was writing was there. Scarcely knowing how he did it, Skye dropped from the loft to the floor of the barn and in the same motion hurried to the workbench.

Turning the pages of the notebook, Bernard Skye was astounded. It was like coming upon a crude effort to counterfeit fifty-dollar bills. Ober had mimicked Webster's hand closely enough so that it could easily fool a nonexpert, Skye granted him that, but far more interesting was what Ober had written. What guts the guy had. To produce what looked to be a manuscript of Howard Webster! The motive could only be gain but why hadn't he saved himself the trouble and just stolen a genuine manuscript? The entries in the notebook were obviously patterned on Webster's novella, only Ober was proposing a different ending. The wrong body had been burned. It was Ober who had died and been cremated by Webster who then had simply disappeared. And then Skye saw the significance of the notebook. My God! Did Ober imagine that he was the late Howard Webster, returned from self-imposed exile, ready to take possession of all that was rightfully his?

The sheer ambition and daring of the plan excited Skye's admiration. Obviously there was a lot more to Ober than the curator of the Webster Library had begun to guess. Why hadn't he invoked the help of Bernard Skye? Perhaps he intended to, once he had completed the work he was engaged upon.

Skye remained in the barn, sunk in grudging admiration of Ober's presumptuous plan. His initial skepticism went as he imagined himself colluding with Ober. Felicia would be the hardest nut to crack, of course. Imagine convincing a daughter that some drunken tramp was her father!

The sound of the car startled him. He mustn't let Ober

know he had discovered his planned hoax. He scrambled up into the loft and ran in a crouch to the back door. He held it high and let himself drop. He hit the ground painfully but limped around the far side of the barn so that he got between the house and barn as Ober was emerging from the car. Skye went to him as quickly as his aching ankles permitted, certain Ober would think he had just emerged from the house.

"Did you get everything?" he asked, beginning to remove bags from the back seat.

"Thorwalds were out of double-A batteries."

"Damn!" The batteries had been merely an excuse to prolong Ober's stay in town.

He turned to face Ober and for the first time really looked at him. A boozy old guy who dared to imagine himself claiming to be the dead poet Howard Webster could not be all bad.

"How about a beer, Ober?"

"I'll take a rain check."

And sure enough he headed out to the barn. With that kind of discipline the guy could be a real writer.

5

Sea and Sardinia? I never thought of the connection.
The freighter stopped at Cagliari and I was weary of a
rolling existence among the smells of oil and the sea.
The crew left me to myself, I might have been the
ancient mariner. Sitting motionless in my cabin, disin-
clined to write or read or even to pursue consecutive
thought, I let whatever came to mind come to mind.
With time I took an almost sensual pleasure from these
hours of passive thinking. Was this perhaps what was
meant by meditation? No wonder monks gave up the
world for the contemplative life. Doctor Johnson said that
marriage has its pains but celibacy has no pleasures. He
was right about marriage, God knows, but clearly he had
no acquaintance at all with the joys of chastity.

Looking back now, my thinking is analytical. I find
myself inclined to wonder about the role the Song of
Songs played in the lives of the great mystics. Bernard
of Clairvaux. But at sea and then ashore on Sardinia I

did not think about my thinking, desired no commentary on the text of my musings. I aspired to be a blank slate on which the world could write whatever it would.

Phoenician, Carthaginian, Roman—Sardinia seemed a vast cemetery, but what land does not if we think of the generations of humans who have moved across a landscape, some ceasing to move and given back to the earth, others passing on to their eventual burial place? Memories of the blazing pyre on which I had placed Ober's body came and went but I did not wonder what the sequel had been. The fire might have gone out and his still identifiable body found. A search would have begun for me in that case, I suppose, suppose now I mean, I did not think such thoughts in Sant'Antioco.

Sant'Antioco. When Virgil describes the Elysian Fields he must have had Italian landscapes in mind, however unconsciously, maybe the countryside around Naples, but Sant'Antioco would have served him better. As a Catholic, don't I believe in a New Jerusalem? Such imaginings seem proper to fundamentalists, but what was the phrase at the Mass? Christ has died, Christ is risen, Christ will come again. It sounds like roadside warnings in the South. Jesus Is Coming. All Christians believe that, believe that souls will get their bodies back again, and live on a new earth. Make it Sant'Antioco, that's my suggestion. Travel brochures for the next world. Spend Your Eternity in Sant'Antioco.

God knows I would have been willing to. What would I have done when my money ran out? I never thought of it. Living in the moment, ignoring thoughts of past or future, my life mimicked eternity. Without change to measure there is no time. The year and more I spent in Sant'Antioco were the happiest time of my life.

Yet I remained a stranger. Even in the hotel where I stayed I was treated to the end as someone who was there for the night and would be gone forever in the morning. The shaded street I walked along day after day, passing shops and faces that grew familiar, did not accept me as permanent. Perhaps lands that have been invaded again and again learn to preserve a distance from intruders. Not that I sought inclusion in the local life. And what was life there? Birth, copulation and death. And going to Mass. In May there were lengthy Marian devotions before the daily Mass, and I sat there in that big chalky church, its windows almost clear glass, a shaft of sun descending pentecostally down a skylight in the middle of the nave, sat there and listened to the murmur of reiterated prayer, borne along by the music of the words as much as their meaning. Now and at the hour of our death.

And what if I had not picked up that tattered, much read magazine in the barber shop? A deed that might so easily not been done. I might at this moment still be in Sant'Antioco, like Lazarus in his winding sheet, unsummoned, still happily among the dead. Statistically it was wildly unlikely that I would have picked up that magazine. I shut it immediately, in the absurd fear that the barber would recognize me as the man in the photographs. But a look in the mirror told me how unlikely that was. Death had aged me. I looked to be the old man that I was. In the magazine, there wasn't a picture of me less than a decade old. Since returning I have proved again and again that the man I am is not identifiable as the poet Howard Webster.

How does one react to the news that one has become famous in absentia? One returns to life, if I am any measure. Thoughts, desires, ambitions that had been dead in me since I walked away from the farm once more marched through me like a conquering army. That The Leaden Echo, written in such haste, should have enjoyed the reception that it did, exhilarated me. That my poetry was once again in print and being read was like hearing a favorable verdict at the general resurrection. What music could be sweeter than the praise heaped on my work, particularly the praise of old enemies and rivals? My first impulse was to cry out, I am alive, I am here, give me your laurels.

A moment's thought, thought of a kind I had not engaged in in Sardinia, told me that I was in a delicate position. All I had to do was think of my old enemies maneuvered into a laudatory stance by my permanent exit to realize that they would not welcome the flesh-and-blood Howard Webster back to the land of the living. What was more important to me, that my work should be read and loved, or that I personally should be the recipient of that reaction and of the wealth that went with it? I decided to stay in Sardinia, safe among the millennia of dead who had earlier laid claim to the island.

But I began to write again. The juices flowed as never before. The "Novena to Sant'Antioco" was the first, technically complicated, chastely simple, the first nonet filling the page as if I were taking dictation.

> Island off an island
> Sant'Antioco
> Where a mixed band
> Of brigands, saints and
> Other dead go,
> Shades in shadow, dust
> To dust. White circling sand
> Measures Antioco,
> Recycling relics of lust.

6

WHEN FELICIA had removed approximately one half of the papers from the farm, she and Frank agreed that the time had come for the announcement of a cache of Webster papers hitherto unknown. It would be made clear that these were papers Felicia had withheld from the Webster Library, that they were considered to be of considerable value and would be of great interest to collectors of Webster memorabilia.

"That should attract the dealers," Frank said approvingly.

"It better. It hasn't been easy getting these together."

They were in Frank's office, the papers she had removed from the farm piled on his desk. Neither of them quite dared believe they were looking at a fortune. And Felicia was the more skeptical of the two.

"I just don't understand why people want old papers. Especially his."

Frank came around the desk and put his arm about her shoulders and tugged her to him. If nothing else, robbing Peter to pay Paul, so to speak, had brought her and Frank close together again. Taking those papers seemed in part to cancel her unintended propelling of her dead father into fame and fortune but she would cancel the cancelation by stirring up new interest in her father.

How could she hate someone of whom she had no clear image? When she did permit a likeness of her father to form in her mind, she realized it was based on a photograph, probably a dust jacket, and was not taken from life. The truth is she had scarcely seen her father since she was a girl and of course he could not possibly have resembled those photographs in later life.

"Selling them is the best revenge," Frank said. He meant the papers.

"You're right."

She shared his relief that the prospect of selling all these papers made up for his stupidity in trusting Hector. But what was the handful of letters Hector had stolen compared with all this?

Cannon the lawyer had called her up as soon as he heard of the sale of Webster letters in New Jersey.

"Were they stolen?"

"Stolen?"

"From the library."

"Why on earth would you think that?"

"Because you gave all your father's literary effects to the Webster Library."

"I gave to the library the papers I gave to the library. Many I retained. Among them the letters my husband sold through a third party."

"Frank sold them?"

It annoyed her that these questions suggested she had anything to explain to Cannon and when he said that it had been his understanding that she had set up the foundation and the library precisely because she wanted a place to put all her father's literary remains, she stopped him.

"I have no idea what you did or did not think, but I don't see why you expect me to comment on it either way."

How exhilarating to feel that she had the upper hand on Cannon at last. He had outfoxed and outmaneuvered her in the management of the foundation, but he would shortly learn that he was presiding over a considerably diminished treasure trove. When the papers she had repossessed were put on the market, the holdings of the Webster Library would diminish in importance, not least because what she had left at the farm was of less interest than what she had taken. With the notable exception of the manuscript of *The Leaden Echo*. Cannon had parlayed the reiterated claim to having been the boyhood companion of her father into a stranglehold, thanks to Baum's vote, over the dispersal of the income from the Webster Foundation. There was no way in which she could wrest control of *The Leaden Echo* royalties from the foundation, a painful realization, but she could ensure that any future bonanza from her father's estate would be hers alone.

"I expected you to share my shock," Cannon said, his voice sad and accusative.

"There is no cause for shock."

"Not as you explain things, no."

She told him she couldn't talk further and put down the phone, his voice still audible before the connection was broken.

"Cannon," she said to Frank.

"That shit."

"You should have warned me earlier."

"Ha. I did."

"How do we go about selling those papers?"

"Why not contact Hollander?"

"Good idea. Maybe he can tell us where Hector absconded with all that money."

But that bonus would be just that, a bonus, if they made what they hoped from the papers.

7

SKYE HAD never dealt with Cannon before, despite the fact that the lawyer was president of the Webster Foundation. Skye figured the man was a figurehead; Felicia had always made decisions without any suggestion they had to be cleared with the other officers of the foundation. But then Cannon appeared at the farm, shading his eyes in a sort of salute as he tried to peer through the screen door. Skye left him out there while he identified himself and even when he knew who Cannon was he did not regard the man as his employer.

"Pour us a drink," Cannon said, when he settled in a library chair. It was the moment of truth, clearly enough. If Skye obeyed he was acknowledging the other man's authority over him. If he told Cannon where the booze was, help yourself, he was announcing his autonomy.

"Bourbon or Scotch?"

"Scotch. Ice, no water."

What the hell, why play games? Giving a man a drink was not the moral equivalent of kissing his ass. Then why did it feel like it was?

"You read about the Webster letters sold in New Jersey?" Cannon said after he tasted his drink and turned small eyes set close over the rodent nose on Skye.

"Yes, I did."

"Were you surprised?"

"At the price?" Skye shrugged. "Not really."

"That isn't what I meant."

Skye waited, but Cannon was waiting too. Another moment of truth. "What did you mean?"

"My first thought was that those were letters that belonged here."

Careful, careful. One interpretation of Cannon's remark was that Skye had known of and even colluded in the sale of letters that were part of the collection he had been hired to look after. Memories of Princeton and his humiliating separation from that project were suddenly vivid in his mind. Dear God, he could not go through that sort of thing again. Particularly when he was innocent.

"I spoke with Mrs. Leamon however and she assured me the letters were not among the papers she donated."

Skye managed not to heave a sigh of relief. "She ought to know."

"Yes, indeed. But as an officer and trustee of the foundation I would like independent verification. Have you completed the cataloguing Clinton started?"

"I've been working on the library. At Mrs. Leamon's suggestion."

"You mean the cataloguing of the papers hasn't proceeded beyond what Clinton did?"

"That's right."

"Why would she divert you to the books?"

"I suppose because she didn't like the way the cataloguing was going."

"Oh?"

"I'm going to start over from scratch once I'm done in here."

"Redo what Clinton did?"

"That's all been erased anyway."

"Erased!"

Cannon lurched in his chair, spilling Scotch on his knee, but he just clamped a hand over it and focused his little eyes on Skye.

"Mrs. Leamon suggested I devise a new system, less cumbersome than the one Clinton came up with. Of course I agreed but, as I said, she wanted me first to catalogue Webster's books."

"If Clinton's records are erased, how can we know what is in the collection and what isn't?"

"Well, of course, Clinton's catalogue wouldn't answer that question, except in part."

"How can we know the letters sold in New Jersey were not in the collection?"

"Oh, they couldn't have been."

"Why not?"

"How would they ever have gotten to New Jersey?"

This is what fishing must be like, playing the catch once it is hooked, letting out a little line then reeling it in. It gave Skye a sense of power to know that he had backed up on diskettes Clinton's catalogue before erasing it from the hard disk. Clearly Cannon suspected that Felicia had taken back the letters she had donated and put them on the market through an intermediary. Maybe he was right. God knows she had taken a bundle of things away with her each time she visited. The letters were not in Clinton's catalogue— Skye had checked to make certain—but that did not mean they weren't among the things Felicia had carried off.

"They could have been stolen," Cannon said after a full minute of exasperated silence.

"Hey, wait a minute. I'm responsible for these papers."

"Take it easy. I'm not accusing you. But tell me this. Is it possible that Felicia might have taken those letters from here?"

Skye feigned shock and incomprehension. "If she did, and I'm not saying she did, wouldn't she have had every right to?"

"No!" Cannon closed his eyes and shook his head vigorously three times. "If she gave those letters to the foundation, they are no longer her property. As president of the foundation I have legal responsibility for the papers donated to the foundation. It is in that capacity that I put these questions to you."

"Weren't you given printouts of Clinton's catalogue?"

"No."

Skye had figured as much. Felicia had kept them or destroyed them, probably the latter after she had begun to raid the files at the farm. Her plan was clear enough now. Cannon was a pain in the ass who had somehow gained control of the Webster Foundation and now Felicia was making that less of an accomplishment by repossessing her father's papers. And not to set up another library, Skye was sure.

Two days later his guess was verified when Hollander in New Jersey announced that he was representing Howard Webster's daughter in the disposition of some of her father's most important papers. A little smile formed on Skye's lips. A ship he had once thought he descried on the distant horizon when working on the Princeton project was coming into port for sure.

BOOK THREE

BOOK THREE

1 | PART ONE |

WESSEL THE city editor told her about the papers Felicia had consigned to the dealer in New Jersey and joked about flooding the market, but Aran managed to keep her cool until she was in the ladies where she lit a cigarette and soundlessly pronounced all the obscenities she could think of. That lousy bitch! After claiming to give all her father's papers to the goddam Webster Foundation, invented to foil Aran, Felicia now announced that she had an attic full of papers she forgot to give to the Webster Library. These papers, supposedly the best, she would sell. Well, by God, any money she got from those Aran intended to share. Flooding the market, Wessel had said. Imagine the reception she would get now if she tried to sell the things Howard was working on.

She left the *Journal* without even punching out. She was burning her bridges. It was all or nothing now. She had been a fool to accept more or less passively the games Felicia had been playing with Howard's stuff. Well, the best way to stop her was for Howard Webster himself to step forward and put an end to this trafficking in his papers. Howard could lay claim to all the money that had been earned from his work, the farm and papers would be his again, there would be a definitive break with Felicia. Aran could even imagine Howard and herself settled down on the farm again, glad to have a second chance.

There was no message from Howard on her answering device but of course he would not yet have heard of what Felicia had done. Aran realized she had to be the one to tell him and that meant driving out to the farm.

On the way, she thought of Howard diligently producing new work so that the two of them could do what Felicia had now done. She was stealing their thunder. In the fields flanking the road spiky stalks of last summer's corn created an unshaven look. When they were married, in the morning when he first awoke, she had loved to rub Howard's bristly face against the grain. What an odd thing a beard is. When Howard emerged smooth-faced from the bathroom later he seemed to have scraped away ten years. The beard with which he had returned from Sardinia was silken but gray, giving him the look of an old man. Well, what else was he at sixty-one? She had not recognized him, no one would have recognized him. Yet in recent days, despite the beard, he had seemed less old. Because he was writing again? If he kept it up he would soon be recognizable as the Howard Webster of a few years ago.

When she turned in the drive at the farm, splashes of forsythia brightened one side of the road but the lawn leading up to the house had a dead, khaki look to it still. She drove around the house and parked well short of the barn. When she turned off the motor, she rolled down the window and sat as silence descended. Almost imperceptibly at first the country sounds began, the creak of dry branches overhead, the caw of crows, a rhythmic drip of water over a leaf-clogged drain. And soon from far off the vague roar of traffic. How she had loved and hated the solitude of this place. She got out of the car and eased the door closed. High above, the contrails of a jet turned fluffy in a pale blue sky. She waited by the car, but Howard did not appear. Then she noticed that the barn door was ajar.

He had told her where he worked, oddly proud of the primitive setting and austerity.

"Optimum circumstances are the death of art, Aran. That's why the farm was a mistake. At last I would have the kind of setting I always wanted, the perfect place to work. And of course I did nothing."

He could say that with gusto because once again he was writing. But was it true he'd done nothing while living at the farm? She seemed to remember him constantly at work.

"You wrote *The Leaden Echo*," she reminded him, but this had the effect of making him frown.

At the barn, she called out before opening the door.

"Howard? It's Aran."

She stepped inside and her eyes were drawn to the puddle of light falling on the workbench. He turned in silhouette.

"You won't believe what Felicia has done."

He moved into the light then and she saw it was Bernard Skye.

"Did you say Howard?"

"What are you doing here!"

"I live here. Who'd you think you were speaking to?"

"You live in the barn?"

What an insolent bastard he was. Aran turned and left the barn, not certain what she should do. Skye had heard her address Howard and she had no intention of being quizzed about that. He came out into the gray afternoon light.

"Why did you call me Howard?"

She looked at him with a half smile, then covered her face. "For a moment I thought you were . . ." And she began to sob.

Perhaps this is what is meant by poetic inspiration. Aran

felt that she was playing a role someone else had written, a perfect defense against Skye's curiosity, a plausible explanation. A woman once married to a dead poet comes to where they had lived together and seeing in silhouette a man at her husband's workbench has the momentary illusion that it is her husband. Crazy of course, but touching. Skye took her arm and led her deferentially to the house.

"I'll make you some tea."

"I'd rather have a drink."

"We'll see if Ober has left us any."

Howard was in the library, drunk as a lord, a bottle of bourbon on the table beside his chair, a glass gripped in his hand. She knew the pose too well. Portrait of a poet determined to get drunk. His beard looked scruffy and unattractive: it aged him. He hardly glanced at her before splashing more bourbon into his glass and raising it to his lips. If the past was any guide, he would be out of commission for days after he finally stopped pouring liquor into himself and he still seemed far from that point. The urgency with which she had come to the farm now seemed foolish. Other, more repellent memories of their life together here came and she wondered how she had imagined living an idyll with him here once they had marketed the new manuscripts.

"What can I fix you?" Skye asked.

"Maybe I will have tea."

"Good idea." Skye looked with disgust at Ober. "You mistook me for Webster, but our friend here has begun to think he really is the man. Apparently he even wants to drink like him."

When Skye went into the kitchen, Aran knelt next to Howard's chair.

"What on earth are you doing?"

"The sonofabitch stole it." He sprayed these sibilants as he spoke in what was meant to be a whisper.

"I'll tell you all about it," Skye called from the kitchen.

Howard heaved himself up from his chair, threw a fierce look toward the kitchen and reeled into the study, slamming the door behind him. He had taken the bourbon along. Aran went into the kitchen where Skye had just put the kettle on. He nodded toward the table and she sat.

"Ober's been trying to forge Webster documents."

She made a face. "I don't believe it."

"He began drinking when I told him I'd discovered what he has been up to."

"Have you heard what Felicia Leamon has done?"

He hadn't. He sat across the table from her, attentive, untrustworthy, waiting. Aran told him of the deal with the man in New Jersey and as she talked Skye began to nod, smiling, as if she were telling him what he already knew.

"She's been stealing this place blind ever since I got here."

"You're supposed to be the curator!"

"She hired me."

"You've seen her taking things from the collection here?"

He nodded. "Of course it's just my word against hers."

The kettle began to whistle and he pushed back from the table. "Care for some toast?"

Why not? He poured the water into the pot and put it on the table to steep and then put bread in the toaster. Aran could sense that he was plotting as he performed these tasks. He had told her about Felicia and the point was, why?

"Aran, you and I have to write ourselves into Felicia's deal."

"Oh sure. And how are we going to do that?"

He offered her a plateful of buttered toast. "I think I have a way."

2

FROM HOLLANDER'S study the buildings of the university were visible in the middle distance but just behind the house traffic roared past, considerably diminishing the sense of rural solitude. By contrast, Howard Webster's farm seemed the back of beyond. But then Hollander did not want to be too far from the cultural currents on which he plied his trade. Like countless other individuals and enterprises, he had put his Princeton postmark to good effect, creating the impression of a connection with the university. The town was jammed with hangers-on, people wanting to be considered part of the academic community and of course ignored by it. John O'Hara, some of whose papers Hollander had handled, had a classic case of Princetonitis, hoping to derive from proximity to the campus and the Institute for Advanced Study the éclat he felt the lack of a degree denied him. Thus the upwardly mobile lapsed Catholic began to ape the mannerisms of the Wasp. It was a subject rich in irony, Holly thought, his Jewishness protecting him from that temptation at any rate. It was those with whom he dealt who were meant to be impressed by the Princeton association. As for himself, he could have been content in Asbury Park.

Listening to the dealer, being exempted from the presumed snobbishness of his clientele, Frank wondered if this spiel was meant to devalue the suitcase full of Webster papers he had just shown the dealer. As he spoke, Hollander began to move things from the suitcase to the top of his desk. He fell silent and he studied a sheaf of pages.

"My God! This is the holograph of the 'Baraboo Elegies.' " He glanced at Frank, as if to cancel the effect of this enthusiasm.

"Everything there is first-order stuff."

Hollander nodded, sat and pushed his chair away from the desk so his view of Frank would not be obstructed by the papers.

"Tell me about these."

"What would you like to know?"

"To whom do they belong?"

"My wife."

"The daughter of Howard Webster?"

"Yes."

"My understanding was that she'd created a foundation and then a library to which she donated all her father's papers."

"What she gave turned out not to be all."

Hollander waited and Frank told him of a small green metal steamer trunk that had been stored in the attic of their home. Felicia had assumed it contained only her mother's effects and at the time of the founding of the library had ignored it.

"The papers donated to the library are those already at the farm."

"I see. And why has she decided to sell these rather than put them with the others?"

This part of the story was easier. He told Hollander how Cannon had maneuvered himself into a position of control of the foundation, thwarting Felicia's efforts to establish fellowships for poets and generally souring her on the whole notion of the foundation and the library.

"She has no intention of turning over any more papers to Cannon's control."

Hollander turned in his chair to take a half-smoked cigar from a large ashtray on the desk. He had offered Frank a cigar earlier as an excuse for lighting his own and now, before relighting it, he asked Frank if he was sure he wouldn't like a cigar.

"I'll have a cigarette."

"Oh, thank God. I can't trust a man who doesn't smoke."

"Then you must not trust many people."

Hollander's full lips formed a smile even as he puffed on his cigar, filling the study with clouds of bluish smoke.

Frank produced Felicia's letter, expressing her desire that Hollander represent her in disposing of those papers of her father's that she had lately discovered in the attic. Attached to the letter was a nine-page description of the papers. Hollander made little whistling sounds as he went through the list.

"I will print a brochure, very attractive, very expensive. I think an auction will be the best way to proceed. I will set minimal prices and we will go from there."

"Do you have a rough idea . . ."

"How much?" Hollander studied the wet end of his cigar. "Let us just say that we are all going to be very pleased, and very rich."

Frank was already back in Milwaukee when Hollander issued a press release, discreetly, announcing the availability of Howard Webster papers and the imminent publication of a catalogue. The auction would be held in Hollander's gallery on Nassau Street. Felicia was radiant with delight at the message he had brought from Princeton.

"How does he define rich?"

"How do we?"

For Frank wealth meant getting out from under the mountain of bad debts he had accrued from his association with Hector. Just to start off even again was his current idea of nirvana. Untrammeled by debt, his income was more than sufficient for a comfortable life. To pay off those debts and get out from under had been their initial motivation for wanting to sell Webster papers but Hollander promised a good deal more than that, and it was only fitting that Felicia take pleasure in it. He did not report to her on the exchange he had had with Hollander about Hector.

"You remember the Webster letters that were brought to you a month ago?"

Hollander rolled his eyes. "If I had only known they were just a swallow announcing this springtime flood." He waved his cigar toward the desk.

"Have you been in touch with Hector since?"

"Your intermediary?"

Frank made a face. "I haven't heard from him myself."

Hollander carefully rolled ash from his cigar. "What are you saying?"

"That he took the money and ran."

Hollander let his head roll from side to side as he emitted a small theatrical moan. "I had an inkling about that man. If it hadn't been for your letter and the confirming phone call I would never have dealt with him."

"Dealing with him is invariably costly."

Hollander had pulled himself up to his desk where he put his cigar in the ashtray and began to twirl through a Rolodex. When he found what he wanted he tipped back his head to look through the lower lens in his glasses. "Here we are. As a routine matter I asked him for personal references. I wanted two, he gave me only one." Hollander looked at Frank over his glasses. "He wanted to use you as one reference."

"Who is the other one?"

"Do you know a Mrs. Metzger?"

Frank's laugh was delayed. "She wouldn't give him much of a reference." He took the card Hollander had removed from the Rolodex. "Mrs. Metzger is my secretary."

"I told you I didn't trust him. Even though he did smoke a cigar with me. It was your letter plus speaking with you on the phone that persuaded me to go ahead. You saw none of the money?"

"How much was there?"

"Net, after my fee?" He took from the drawer of the desk a ledgerlike notebook and opened it. "Fifty thou."

"Ouch."

"You mustn't let him get away with it. If you like, I can have inquiries made . . ."

"I'll take care of it."

What he had meant by that was difficult to say. He would gladly offer up all his losses if the papers he had turned over to Hollander would, in the dealer's words, make them rich.

The future looked unclouded indeed until Bernard Skye showed up at his office.

"Congratulations on this," Skye said, holding up one of Hollander's brochures.

Frank nodded. If congratulations were in order he wasn't sure Skye was the one to offer them.

"I've been on the phone to Holly. His hopes for the auction are high, and believe me he's seldom wrong."

Holly? "We have every confidence in him."

"Of course there's no way he could know that the papers were repossessed from the library." Skye smiled conspiratorially. "Don't worry. I put no bee in his bonnet."

A minute before Bernard Skye had been an almost stranger and, although Frank was mildly annoyed that the curator should interrupt his office routine, he had felt no animosity. Now he was filled with hatred for the man. The prospects that had reduced his consumption of Maalox, put a smile on his lips and spring to his step, that had brought new warmth and intimacy to his marriage, were threatened by this odious man with his insinuating smile. For the first time in his life Frank knew what it was like to want to kill. Not even Hector's perfidy had elicited such a reaction from him. Hector had always retained the saving grace of really believing in whatever crazy scheme he brought to Frank. Skye was a cynic, a parasite, unworthy to be called a man.

"What are you getting at?"

"A three-way split. I watched your wife take papers from the farm. That's no skin off my nose so long as I'm part of it. There's no need for Holly to get nervous about whether these papers are really yours to offer."

Frank opened the drawer of his desk and brought out a pack of cigarettes. He took one and threw the package on the desk. The world was in suspense until he lit up.

"Can I have one of those?"

"You smoke?"

"On festive occasions."

So much for Hollander's theory.

3

"YOU WON'T get away with this," Cannon said on the phone. He kept running out of breath before finishing sentences.

"Mr. Cannon," Felicia said, relishing the formality, "this conversation is pointless. I don't need your approval let alone your permission to turn my father's papers over to a dealer."

"You do if the papers belong to the Webster Foundation."

"I concede that. But these papers are mine."

"Felicia, I'll read the relevant portion of your bequest again if you like. In it you give to the foundation all your father's papers. All. That is quite explicit."

"All that I gave, yes."

"That is not what it says."

"I could not give what I did not know I had."

"Felicia, I am confident that any judge would construe matters as I do. You turned over to the foundation all your father's papers, known or unknown. There was no inventory list to restrict the range of your gift."

"That's lawyer talk. Do you think anyone is impressed with such niggling argument? Any sensible person will understand that I gave what I gave and did not give what I did not give. I had no obligation to give anything. The idea for the foundation was mine."

"It was a vindictive idea."

"That you wormed your way into control is neither here nor there."

"What happened to the catalogue Clinton made?"

"Did Clinton make a catalogue?"

"You know he did. And you ordered Bernard Skye to destroy it. That enabled you to steal papers from the Webster Library . . ."

She hung up on him. What an insufferable man he was. She had been confident she could handle Cannon, she had taken too much of his insolence not to relish this chance to parry his every thrust, but the mention of Bernard Skye was another matter. Had Skye reported to Cannon her orders to clear the computer's hard disk? If so, Skye might also have told Cannon that she had walked off with a significant fraction of the papers stored at the farm.

But Felicia doubted this. If she knew Cannon he would have led off with that knowledge, not held it back until after he mentioned the destruction of Clinton's catalogue. But obviously he had been told of the catalogue. If nothing else this reminded her of the fact that Skye *could* inform Cannon or anyone else that she had taken papers from the farm. She had made no serious effort to conceal what she was doing; she had acted in the conviction that she could not be accused of stealing what was rightly hers anyway. If she had taken the papers home without the intention of retaining them, her situation would look different. But she was about to make a great deal of money from the sale of the papers, and the fact that she had bequeathed "her father's papers" to the foundation was undoubtedly relevant. Hence the story Frank had passed on to Hollander. These papers were a new find, unrelated to those she had given the foundation.

The destruction of Clinton's catalogue had of course been crucial. Thank God she had thought of that as step one. Even if she were accused of taking papers from the farm— and it continued to rankle her that taking what had been hers should be thought of as theft—there was no way anyone could prove that the papers Frank had turned over to Hollander had been taken from the farm. So she was not bothered by Cannon's claim that her original gift included all and every Webster paper, presently at the farm or not. If things really were as she claimed, she was not in the least vulnerable. Of course the alleged attic discovery involved papers she had taken from the farm. But only she could know that the papers listed in Hollander's elegant brochure were identical with papers that had been in the library.

"Bernard Skye came to see me," Frank said.

"Oh?"

"He wants one third of the profits from the sale of the papers."

Felicia laughed. "Why not half? Why not all?"

"He claims he saw you removing papers from the farm."

"Does he? Can he identify those papers?"

"Felicia, this could be serious."

"I don't see how. Bernard Skye's reputation is tainted. That's why I hired him. His unsupported word isn't worth a hill of beans. The first thing he did as curator was erase the catalogue Clinton had been making."

"He said you told him to do that."

"Nonsense," she said, confidently occupying a make-believe world. "I told him not to feel bound by what Clinton had done. If he wanted to start over from scratch that was all right with me. Meanwhile, I suggested he concentrate on cataloguing the books at the farm. In any case, he erased Clinton's work, one consequence of which is that there is no way of telling what papers were at the farm and what were not."

Frank's worried expression faded as she spoke and then he came to take her in his arms. Felicia was filled with a sudden sense of power. She had demonstrated to herself that she could handle Cannon; what Frank saw as a threat from Bernard Skye, she had easily shown to be nothing of the sort. No accident, that, given the care with which she had hired him. She had wanted a curator who would pose no obstacles to her intention of pillaging the papers she had mistakenly lost legal control of. Her one regret was that she had acceded to Skye's request for a CD player. The ass had taken that as an admission of worry on her part, an effort to placate him.

The following afternoon she drove to the farm to confront Skye. How exhilarating it was to deal with men from such an advantageous position.

Skye sauntered onto the porch when she parked the car by the barn. He stood, legs apart, thumbs hooked in his belt, smiling as she came toward him. Perhaps he thought his visit to Frank was about to bear the hoped-for fruit.

"Good afternoon."

"Why aren't you working?"

His smile wavered then firmed. "Just thought I'd greet the boss."

"Let's go inside. I want an account of how you've been spending your time as curator."

It was an off-balance Skye who preceded her into the house, impatiently waved ahead when he stepped aside to let her enter. Felicia was here in the role of Skye's employer and was not about to let him forget it.

"I've got coffee on," he said, his tone altered, the smile gone.

She ignored this and sailed on into the study, where she settled herself at the desk.

"Have you completed the cataloguing of the books in the library yet?"

"I wouldn't say I've completed it." He searched her face to discover how he was meant to take this uncharacteristic arrival. Perhaps he was remembering her suggestions that he need not hurry through the task.

"What *would* you say?"

"I've got a good start."

"How long have you been here?"

"Oh, come on. What is this? You know how long I've been here."

"Indeed I do. The question is what am I paying you for?"

He sat down, tipped back in his chair and tried to resume his insolent manner. "Cannon tells me he's my employer, not you."

"If you imagine I am going to discuss matters internal to the administration of the foundation with you, you are very much mistaken."

"Cannon was willing enough."

"Let me see the progress you've been making on cataloguing these books."

Skye stirred in his seat and smiled. "I'd rather talk about the papers you've put on the market."

"So my husband tells me. Perhaps we should talk about your previous experience in cataloguing. Perhaps we should talk about the Princeton project."

Skye looked at her in injured disappointment. "Why did you hire me?"

"You mustn't assume I knew all about you before I did. But I am glad we are clear as to who did hire you. Mr. Skye, a bit of advice. You have an opportunity to remain in your position here. You have the chance to acquire an entry in your employment record that will do something toward canceling what happened in Princeton. It's entirely up to you."

The record he produced of his cataloguing was risible and she told him as much. She put him on probation. Unless he demonstrated within the next two weeks that he was seriously engaged on the tasks for which he had been hired, he would be dismissed and the reasons for it would be made available to any future employer. Skye sat through this in seething silence. When she was done, he rose and advanced toward her. It was all Felicia could do not to push back from the desk.

"Move."

"What do you want?"

"Something from the desk drawer."

She pushed back and opened the drawer and immediately his hand swooped to take something from it.

"What is that?"

"The first thing I intend to enter in the cataloguing of the materials here at the farm."

He left the room and Felicia remained where she was. It would have been infra dig to go after him to see what it was he had snatched from the desk drawer. After five minutes, she rose and went briskly through the library on her way to the kitchen. There she poured a cup of coffee and stood looking at Skye busy at the computer. Coffee in hand she went to stand beside him. On the screen this legend appeared.

Blue cloth-covered notebook, 5" x 7.5", no cover markings. Contents 32 pages holograph Howard Webster, alternative version The Leaden Echo.

It was a description of what he had taken from the desk in the study. Felicia picked up the notebook and opened it. The handwriting was unmistakable. The first few entries justified Skye's description. The realization grew on her that what she held was more valuable than all the other papers she had carried away. Imagine this being published and enjoying a sale comparable to the earlier version of the novella . . .

"When did you find this?"

"Oh, Clinton found it. It's in his catalogue."

"I don't believe you."

"One thing you should know. I made a backup copy of Clinton's catalogue. Twelve diskettes."

"I don't believe you."

"They are in a safe-desposit box in the village bank. I had a hunch it would be to my advantage to make a copy. Given my experience since working in Princeton, I was naturally curious why you should hire me."

He turned away and began to plink away at the computer keys. Felicia's grip on the notebook tightened. She wanted so badly to walk out of here with this second version of her father's story that it required a great act of will to remain. How would it be possible to confiscate this notebook and simply counter with derision and denials when Skye gave his version? Two things stopped her. First was the mention of the backup copy of Clinton's catalogue. That could be a bluff but if not it jeopardized much more than this notebook. Second, as to the notebook, it would be impossible to maintain that her father had given it to her or left it with her since it must be the last thing he wrote.

"Checkmate?" Skye asked, without turning from the computer.

"We'll see," Felicia said in even tones and went out to her car.

Standing in the open door of the barn was the old tramp Ober. Felicia detoured from her car and went to him.

"What do you know of a second version of my father's novella *The Leaden Echo?*"

The man reeked of booze. He studied her with blood-red eyes as if he had to compose what he said before daring to voice it.

"I know it's better than the first version."

"Then you've seen it?"

"I was there when your father wrote it."

Two hours later, in Milwaukee, she was telling Philip Knight and his enormous brother what had recently tran-spired with Cannon and Bernard Skye.

4

PHILIP HAD been about to answer Aran's call when Felicia showed up at the hotel.

"Are you still working for me, Mr. Knight?"

The message from Aran was that she wanted to engage his professional services and it was tempting to tell this haughty woman that he was no longer available. But taking Aran as a client would be too much like ambulance chasing whereas it could be argued, or at least believed in the privacy of his own mind, that anything he did for Felicia would be a continuation of previous employment. Besides, he had the not negligible advantage that she had come to him.

"Yes."

She actually sighed and sank into a chair. "Then I can rely on confidentiality."

He felt no need to tell her that far from being obliged to conceal anything untoward she might tell him he was legally obliged to inform the police. Surely the daughter of Howard Webster had not come to him to devulge felonies.

But that was precisely the burden of her story. After legally giving her father's papers to the Webster Foundation she had proceeded to steal them back again, or at least a significant portion of them, and consigned them to Hollander for sale. She had toughed it out with Cannon when he accused her of this and had thought she was succeeding in the same way with Bernard Skye before he announced the backup copy of Clinton's catalogue.

"I don't believe him, of course. But I have to be sure."

"Ask him to produce it."

She tipped her head to one side. "Bernard Skye is not presently in a mood to accommodate me."

"I'll see what I can do."

Philip felt uneasy and was not sure he liked having Roger here, witnessing what was being said. Felicia had just confessed to theft and fraud, thereby putting a licenced private investigator in an untenable position. Philip had survived untenable positions in the past and was willing to see what he might do to find out if Skye did indeed have a safe-deposit box. But he did not like having Roger privy to such things.

"There's more," Felicia said.

Philip waited. What could be worse than the possibility that proof existed that the papers Felicia had given Hollander were in fact the property of the Webster Foundation?

"Skye has found a later version of *The Leaden Echo.*"

At the mention of yet another unknown literary effort of Howard Webster, Roger nearly rolled off the couch which served him as a chair since by settling onto its middle cushion he spilled over onto the rest, almost wedged between the armrests.

"Have you seen it?"

"Yes."

"It's authentic?"

"It's almost identical to the notes on which the published version was based."

"How long is it?"

Felicia might be as annoyed as she liked about Roger's taking over the questioning, but it was obvious he was not to be denied. After several minutes engaged in a rocking motion, that tipped him ever further forward, Roger suddenly heaved himself from the couch and began to move rapidly and out of control across the room. Philip leapt to his feet and brought his brother to a halt before he upended Felicia.

"Thirty-two pages," she said, looking at the two brothers with apprehension.

"But that's as long as the notes for the novella."

"These are notes for a different version."

"You left them at the farm?"

She looked demurely at Philip. "The notebook belongs to the foundation."

Roger, steadied physically, was still emotionally off balance. Obviously the discovery of that notebook took precedence over everything else. Philip was not disappointed to be diverted from the question of Felicia's purloining of her father's papers. Given the fact that she was the heir, it seemed a diminished kind of theft, though theft it undoubtedly was. Did a woman's prerogative to change her mind apply here? Certainly Cannon's usurpation of the determining role among the officers of the foundation, reducing the poet's daughter to the status of an ineffective minority of one, was a mitigating circumstance. Philip would not characterize himself as a man able to predict what juries and judges might do, but he found it difficult to envision Felicia being punished let alone imprisoned for repossessing her father's papers from a family foundation that had been taken over by a man as dubious as Cannon.

"Who else saw the notebook beside you and Skye?"

"He wouldn't dare steal it," Felicia cried.

The suggestion made Roger tremble with rage.

"Oh, and there's also Ober. He saw my father writing it."

Propped against the wall, Roger wanted every detail of her conversation with Ober and was not put off by Felicia's remark that the man had been roaring drunk at the time, scarcely able to speak coherently.

"But you believed him."

"Yes."

"Then who cares how drunk he is?"

For the next hour, Felicia had to repeat for Roger every word and every movement in her showdown with Skye, its abrupt turnabout when he claimed to have a backup of Clinton's catalogue, the revelation of the notes for a second version of *The Leaden Echo* and finally her encounter with Ober. A disinterested observer would have been excused for thinking that Roger ascribed as much importance to Felicia's few words with the drunken tramp as to the extended encounter with Bernard Skye.

"I want to see that notebook," Roger said finally. "Right away."

To oppose this desire would have been like standing up to a force of nature. Felicia extracted from Philip the promise that he would find out as quickly as possible whether Bernard Skye had a safe-deposit box.

"He said in the village."

"It won't take long to find out if it's there. You realize that even if I find he has such a box, there's no way I can gain access to it."

Even as he said this, he was thinking of ways it might not be true. If the box were in the village bank, Philip had the feeling Ned Bunting could give him an informal inventory of its contents.

"I just have to know," Felicia wailed.

But her curiosity was as nothing compared to Roger's and fifteen minutes later they were on their way to the farm with Roger in the backseat of the rented car, arms akimbo, hands pressed against the side windows in an effort to keep himself balanced.

"If you can get hold of the notebook, I'll leave you at the farm. I want to have a word with Ned Bunting."

Roger nodded, staring past Philip at the road. He was not normally a devotee of speed, indeed by and large he was wholly indifferent to Philip's driving, but now his eyes fairly ate up the road.

5

THE NOTEBOOK had been a bonus, telling her about the backup of Clinton's catalogue would have been more than enough, still Skye thanked his guardian devil for the inspiration to use Ober's crude forgery as a weapon against his oppressor. God, the look on her face when she began to page through that notebook. It had obviously never occurred to her to doubt its authenticity. But then Ober had done a better job than Skye would have dreamt possible, not that it could deceive a professional eye. After she left, he stored the bogus description and picked up the notebook.

"Give me that, you goddam thief!"

Ober stood in the doorway, gripping the frame, drunk as a lord. He weaved as he stood there, as if he might be flung from the planet by centrifugal force. He started toward Skye but stopped, not daring to lose his steadying grip on the doorframe.

"It wouldn't fool anyone, you old fool."

Ober took this as a physical blow. "Then why did you tell her about it?"

"Tell who?"

"Felicia. She came out and asked me about it and I told her."

"Told her you've been holed up in the barn forging a notebook in her father's hand? I'll bet you did."

Ober's mood changed abruptly. A wheezing sound turned into laughter. He stood there, shaking with drunken merriment, tears rolling out of his bloodshot eyes.

"Oh, I wouldn't try to fool someone like you."

He turned himself around, switching hands on the doorframe, and reeled into the kitchen, where he noisily poured himself a cup of coffee.

"Drink it all, you old bastard. Sober up."

It was ridiculous being bothered by the drunken laughter of an old bum like Ober. The whole afternoon had been a kick in the head and Skye was sick of it. He wished now he'd kept clear of Frank Leamon and Cannon, but it had seemed too good a chance to pass up. Felicia had been something else, even though he had the goods on her. Clinton's records would prove she'd been stealing the place blind. But if that came out, so would his past record and he would be doubly damned for being involved in yet another messy situation, no matter that he was innocent. He had been innocent before, at Princeton, except for sins of thought. Are there crimes of thought? There might just as well be, given what a little conversational speculation had done to his career as a paleographer. He might succeed in proving that Felicia had taken papers she'd given to the foundation, but who other than Cannon would really care? Yet everyone would care that a man accused of attempted fraud in Princeton had somehow managed to get the job of curator of the Webster Foundation just when funny things began to happen.

He went into the kitchen where Ober was seated at the kitchen table, slurping coffee from a mug.

"What did you plan to do with that forgery, sell it?"

"Go to hell." But Ober did not sound angry.

"Maybe you could get away with it."

"When I couldn't even fool you?" And the old bastard leered at him. Just then headlights raked the house and advanced up the driveway from the road.

Skye skated across the linoleum floor in stocking feet, his shoes still parked under the computer—he always slipped off his shoes when he used a computer—and got to the kitchen window just in time to see the car go by. Whoever the hell it was, this was after hours. He should have locked up after Felicia left, then he wouldn't have had to take all this guff from Ober.

"Company," Ober burbled happily.

"They've probably come to cart you off for the cure."

"More likely they've come for you, Bernie boy. Felicia probably sent the constabulary for you."

"How about stuffing a sock in your mouth?"

The car had made a semicircle behind the house and now trained its headlights on the back porch. A moment passed before they were extinguished, then all was black. It had seemed only twilight before the car appeared; now it seemed deep night outside. Skye nearly lost his balance when he dashed for the study to slip into his shoes. When he returned and went out onto the back porch, there was still no sign of the visitors. Skye pressed his face against the screen door and peered into the night.

The car door was open and a dim light illumined the interior. The car seemed full of people. But then he saw that one man was trying to help another very fat one from the back seat. Jesus. The Knights. Had Felicia sent those two out here? Skye waited with foreboding while the improbable duo made their way slowly to the house.

"I was just closing up," he said, opening the door.

"Good," cried the fat one. "I want an after-hours look at that notebook."

So she had told them. Laughter from the kitchen decided

Skye against taking care of things fast and telling the Knights the trick he had played on Felicia. The hell with them. The hell with Ober too. Let Roger Knight discover the notebook was the product of the drunken Ober and they could go on from there.

He held the door wide and gave a mock bow as the enormous Roger came sideways through the door.

"Is that coffee I smell?"

"Either that or booze."

"I'd much rather have coffee."

Ober was no longer in the kitchen. He wasn't in the library when they went through it, or in the study. Well, Skye couldn't blame the drunk for getting out of there before his forgery was discovered.

Roger took the notebook when Skye handed it to him and there was a reverent look on the fat man's face. Let him enjoy it while he could. It shouldn't take him long to discover the notebook was a forgery.

Philip Knight stood at the back door. "Who's out in the barn?"

Pale light glowed at the window and a thin sliver from the not quite closed doors lay upon the mud. "Ober spends most of his time out there."

"Funny he should come back."

"This place is like a magnet. Look at you and your brother."

Philip turned and glanced at Skye. "What bank is your safe-deposit box in?"

"She told you about that, did she? Well, she ought to be worried."

"About what?"

"I took the precaution of making a copy of the inventory my predecessor had begun. It will show what papers were here when I took over."

"Good."

"Good? Don't you see what that means? The papers she's selling are ones she gave the foundation."

Philip crossed to the table and sat down. "Yes, I suppose they are. What do you intend to do, accuse her of stealing her father's papers?"

"I made a suggestion to her and her husband."

"Which they refused."

"They'll come around."

Philip Knight shook his head with annoying assurance. "You're wrong about that. You're wrong about everything, Skye. You had a nice position here, why did you ruin it?"

"Me? What did I do? I haven't been stealing the place blind."

"You are trying to blackmail your employer. You just admitted as much to me. Do you want that added to your already shady record?"

Man to man, no bullshit, that was his approach. Bernard Skye felt what little confidence he still had in his ability to lever money out of Felicia fade. Philip Knight was right. His days on this job were numbered, and there wasn't much he could do about it. Felicia would judge his performance inadequate and let him go and what could he say?

"If you know she's selling stolen papers, aren't you an accomplice?"

"Look, I can imagine Cannon pretending indignation about that, but not you."

Cannon. Skye looked at Knight, at a man who seemed to be holding all the cards, and realized he had a trump yet to play. He went to the counter, picked up the phone and put through a call to Milwaukee. Knight watched him with feigned indifference.

"Mr. Cannon? Bernard Skye. I think maybe you ought to get out here right away."

"Now! It's nearly six o'clock."

"Mrs. Leamon has sent a private investigator out here . . ."

"Skye, listen. Don't you let anyone take anything out of there, do you understand me? And I mean anyone."

"Are you coming?"

"I'll be there as fast as I can."

"What's the point of that?" Knight asked.

"I don't like to be ganged up on. I think you ought to talk to the president of the Webster Foundation."

The door of the study opened and Roger emerged, the notebook clutched against him. He shuffled through the library to the kitchen.

"Where is Ober?" he asked Skye but his brother answered.

"Out in the barn."

Roger Knight nodded and shuffled on to the door.

"It's raining, Roger," his brother told him. The fat man waited while his brother got an umbrella for him. There was certainly no sibling rivalry between these two.

"I'll go with you," Philip said.

"No. That's okay. I can make it."

Make it? The fat man sounded as if walking from the house to the barn was an athletic feat. Maybe it is when you're that fat.

6

ROGER PULLED the doors shut behind him when he went into the barn. At the workbench, with the light from the lamp seeming to thin his beard, the old man sat with the fingers of one hand lightly touching the bottle of liquor. Roger shuffled across the dusty floor into the light and lowered himself onto a sawhorse. He took the notebook away from his body, as if he were opening his coat.

"I've been reading this."

The old man was perched on a high stool, the heels of his shoes hooked into the rung.

"You told Felicia you saw Webster writing this?"

He nodded.

"An interesting idea, that it was Ober who died, not Webster. I wonder how the story would have come out."

"We'll never know."

"Oh, I think we do. It amazes me now that I didn't recognize you, despite the change. I am one of your most devoted admirers."

He visibly tried to fight the pleasure the words gave him but could not. In this light and knowing what he now knew, Roger wondered how the man had been able to deceive those who had known him during his late years, especially his daughter.

"That sawhorse can't be very comfortable," Webster said.

"As comfortable as that stool. Tell me what happened." He displayed the notebook again. "Or is this the simple truth?"

"Is truth ever simple?"

Rain dripped from the eaves and the window above the workbench rattled from time to time in a gust of wind as the old man talked like a narrator in Conrad, a measured, even voice to tell a tale that would have seemed sheer fantasy if the speaker was not undoubtedly Howard Webster. The account he gave of Ober's visit was essentially that of the notebook Roger held. Webster's guest had committed suicide and he had burned the body and assumed Ober's identity.

"Leaving a notebook like this behind?"

Webster nodded. Rain washed against the window and Webster took his feet from the rung of the stool and stretched his legs out in front of him. The account he gave of the year and a half in Sardinia seemed a romantic dream, the famous man become anonymous, the dead man moving among the living, a silent poet living from moment to moment. ("Elected silence," Roger murmured.) And then the discovery that his reputation had undergone an astonishing change.

"It had to happen eventually," Roger said. "How tragic that it sometimes takes the death of the poet to draw attention to his achievement."

Webster smiled. "If I had always been so confident I would have been a happier man."

"That it happened as it did is deeply ironic."

"Yes."

"Who actually wrote *The Leaden Echo?*"

"What do you mean?"

"The novella based on the first notebook."

"You will find in the house my manuscript of the novella. The whole written out in my hand."

"Yes, I've seen that. Of course it was written after the publication of the novel."

"The manuscript *after* the publication?"

"You must complete this notebook and tell of your first return here, when Clinton was curator."

"Clinton?"

"The man you killed."

"You have an odd sense of humor."

"My brother and I found the body. Hanging right over there. He had died before you hung him up. Why did you kill him?"

"I didn't kill him!"

"Was it because you have wanted to take credit for his novella? Good as it is, it's only prose. It can never compare with your poetry."

Dear God, what a weakness vanity is, but could one be an artist without it? Poets have often thought of themselves as mere instruments of divine or darker forces, in any case more than themselves, their talent to be cherished more as a gift than an accomplishment. Webster had grown wary when the relief of being recognized had led on to accusation. Didn't he understand the predicament he had put himself in? His eyes widened at Roger's remark on the poetry.

"My poetry is read again because of the success of the novella."

"That is the irony."

"I grant you that prose is not my forte, but why would you imagine the novella is not mine?"

"Because of the manuscript."

"If the printed version does not follow my manuscript exactly . . ."

"No, the oddity is that the manuscript follows the book."

"You're being obscure."

"In the book there are two references to Vice President Quayle in the conversations between you and Ober. You made a serious mistake when you copied them into the manuscript. The same mistake Clinton did when he turned your notebook into a novella."

"And you think that is sufficient . . ."

"At the time of your death or disappearance I doubt that anyone outside his native state knew the senator from Indiana. And not even his mother could have imagined he would be nominated and elected vice president."

"Is that all?"

"Oh, it's more than enough. But there are also literary reasons why you could not have written *The Leaden Echo*."

"Tell me."

"Tell me why you killed Clinton."

"I didn't. No more than I killed Ober. Clinton had some kind of seizure, he slumped in his chair, I thought he was drunk. I was up all night writing out that goddam manuscript . . ." He stopped.

"Go on."

"You're right about that damnable novella. It seemed a small price to pay to ensure that my own work would be read, another arrow in my quiver, a little *jeu d'esprit* before the end. It could be argued that if I had paid attention and noticed what had happened to Clinton, if I had sent for help . . ."

"But you didn't."

"No. Of that I am guilty, a sin of omission. But did I have an obligation to call the local quack?"

"A legal obligation? I don't know."

Webster fell silent. "When I realized that he was dead, it seemed an eerie reprise of Ober. And I had just copied out his phony story of our days and nights together. I wasn't thinking clearly. I hadn't slept in twenty-four hours. It was as if I were planting a clue, hanging him as Ober hanged himself." Webster shook his head. "It was stupid. It was bad art."

"It was a desecration."

"All right, all right. But I killed neither of them, that's the point."

"But what of Mrs. Clinton?"

"I never met the woman."

"The fact that the fingerprints of Howard Webster were found in the car was taken to mean they had been there all along, since before your 'death.' But there is another explanation, isn't there? What danger did she pose to you?"

Webster shook his head rapidly and when he stopped, looked around the barn. "Do you know, our conversation has completely sobered me." He paused. "Roger Knight, I have killed no one. Not Ober, not Clinton, not Clinton's wife."

Roger was willing to accept two-thirds of that denial. Was it Jane's silly claim to have known all about *The Leaden Echo* that had endangered her? Of course her claim was false, but Webster couldn't know that, and after he had copied Clinton's novella he had committed his literary reputation to the authenticity of the novella. If Jane Clinton could jeopardize that, if she knew her husband had written the novella . . .

Webster smiled as Roger developed this line of thought. But before he could respond, the doors behind them opened and Philip looked in.

"We've got company coming, Roger. Skye has summoned Cannon so I called Felicia and her husband. They're all on their way."

"I'll be in."

But Philip had begun to notice the little snuggery Webster had fashioned so he could work in the barn.

"Maybe if Howard Webster had worked out here he would have kept on publishing," Philip said.

"Who knows?" said Roger.

"I'll come in with you," Howard Webster said.

7

NED BUNTING arrived fifteen minutes after Cannon and the Leamons drove in, curious at all the activity going on at this hour of night out at the old Bates place, as the locals persisted in calling the farm Howard Webster had owned for only a decade. Roger had made himself at home in the kitchen, his visit with Ober in the barn seeming to whet his appetite. He began scrambling a dozen eggs and popping sausages into a pan.

"We can eat later," he said to Philip.

Meaning he considered what he was about to have merely a snack to tide him over until they could have a proper meal. When that might be was a good question. Roger had given up the notebook, which quickly became the centerpiece of discussion. Cannon demanded to know why the notebook had never been mentioned before.

"I'll tell you why," Bernard Skye said. He alone was seated as Cannon and Felicia hovered over him like prosecuting attorneys. Frank stood back from a bookshelf, scanning the spines of books as if totally absorbed. Ober was in the window seat, a fifty-yard line spot for whatever contest was about to take place. Having spoken, Skye looked from Cannon to Felicia and back again.

"So tell me," Cannon repeated.

"It was only recently written."

"What the hell is that supposed to mean?"

"It wasn't among the items that Mrs. Leamon might have stolen."

If anything, Felicia seemed relieved to be accused openly by Skye.

"What do you mean, it was just written?"

"It's a forgery."

"Give me that," Felicia said, snatching the notebook and opening it. Her blazing eyes traveled back and forth across the page. She snapped it shut. "This was written by my father."

Skye let out a barking laugh and turned to Ober. "You want to tell them or should I?"

But Ober's eyes were on Felicia. He gave no indication that he had heard Skye.

"Will you cut out the guessing games," Cannon said. "What's wrong with this notebook?"

Skye rose to his feet. "Not a thing. Except that it was written by Ober there, not Howard Webster."

Felicia's laughter filled the room. Frank turned from the bookshelf, a little smile on his face. Cannon looked at Skye with disgust.

Philip took the notebook from Felicia and opened it. He wished Roger was in here so he could settle whether this was the handwriting of Howard Webster. Ober had pushed himself to the edge of the window seat and Philip thought of the snuggery in the barn the old tramp had made for himself.

"Did you write this, Ober?"

"That notebook was written by Howard Webster. I saw him do it."

"Aw, come *on*, Ober!" Skye shouted. "You can't fool experts with something like that." He looked around at the others. "I saw him writing this with my own two eyes. Those entries didn't even exist a few weeks ago."

His voice rose as he spoke, as if to overcome the skepticism with which his words were met.

"Well, this is different anyway," Felicia said, brightly contemptuous. "Or is it? First you deny the notebook is authentic, then you spirit it away . . ."

"I am telling the truth."

"Then I do apologize. That makes this occasion very different."

Skye was beside himself with rage. The woman he had accused was making him look like a fool. Did he see his already damaged career going entirely up in smoke? Emitting an unintelligible sound, he started across the room toward Felicia. Although he did not imagine the curator was a real threat, Philip moved to protect her. Ober too moved, springing from the window seat and rushing to interpose himself between Skye and Felicia Leamon. Philip got hold of Skye's arm and the curator was easily restrained. But Ober, standing before Felicia, his arms stretched to provide maximum defense, began to gasp. The exertion had been too much for him. He looked from face to face as even the gasping stopped and then he pitched forward. Philip pushed Skye aside as Roger suddenly appeared in the kitchen doorway, a napkin tucked into the collar of his enormous polo shirt. It was one of those moments when Roger moved with the grace of a ballet dancer, a very large ballet dancer. He crouched beside the fallen Ober, bent and whispered in his ear. Then, to Philip's surprise, his brother lifted his hand, spoke very rapidly and made the sign of the cross over the fallen Ober.

Epilogue

SOFT WET snow was falling, sticking to the windward side of trees, limning the stark winter branches, bringing the promise of Christmas to Rye. The Knights were in their living room with their guest, the three of them facing the great window that looked out onto the backyard, rendered solemn by the sight of the falling snow and the topic of their conversation. Mulled wine and, in the fireplace, some sputtering logs. Aran held her glass in both hands and sat forward.

"How did you know?"

Roger, who drank no alcohol, was making do with hot chocolate and there were traces of marshmallow on his lips. He looked pleadingly at Philip, wanting him to explain. Roger honestly believed that any reader would spot the flaw but the mention of the vice president in *The Leaden Echo* had been noticed by no reviewer. Roger was far more willing to speak of his conversation with Howard Webster in the barn on the last day of the poet's life.

"You confronted him with what you thought?"

"Yes."

"And he acknowledged it?"

"What else could he do?"

"I have resolved to let him rest in peace," Aran said. "To go on pretending that it was a tramp named Ober who stupidly rose to Felicia's defense and paid for it with his life."

Roger nodded. "But you must expect that sooner or later . . ."

"I don't think anyone would guess. It's too fantastic."

"Maybe you're right."

"What a way to die," she sighed.

"You mean the first time?"

She gave Philip a rueful look. "Your brother is a Catholic, he understands."

"He was absolved of his sins, Aran. You mustn't concern yourself about that."

She sat back. This was not a matter on which she cared to joke.

"I gave him absolution myself."

"You!"

Roger put down his cup and licked his lips. "Yes. In an emergency any baptized Christian can absolve a penitent of his sins. That was clearly an emergency. I acted."

"I never heard of such a thing."

"Oh, I assure you it is quite orthodox. My authority is none other than Etienne Gilson, the great medievalist."

Into the twilight Roger had twaddled on about such arcane lore, but it seemed a consolation to the late poet's third wife. After the unpleasantness at the farm, Felicia had thought better of things, and Aran at last had received an equitable settlement that permitted her to retire from journalism.

"I'm going to Sardinia in the spring," she said, as she prepared to leave. "I want to see the places he saw."

When Philip returned from the station, having seen Aran off on the train to New York, Roger still stood in the window, staring out at the falling snow.

"She's wrong to go to Sardinia, Philip. He never transmuted his stay there into verse. She would be better advised to go to Baraboo and read the elegies there."

"Sardinia sounds more attractive."

Aran's visit had brought back those terrible events in Wisconsin the previous spring and Roger continued to brood over them as they sat at table.

"Sooner or later some scholar will discover that Webster did not write that novella. It really won't harm his reputation. It's the kind of incidental that enhances a literary reputation. Aran would do better to pray that no one discovers that Webster killed Clinton's wife Jane."

"That's pure conjecture, Roger."

"Pure?" Roger asked, giving him a cherubic smile. "Oh, he killed her, there's no doubt of that. It's why I was so intent on absolving him of his sins."

"I hope your theology is sound."

But Roger had at last shaken off his pensive mood and began to heap his plate high with chicken and dumplings. The fire crackled, outside snow fell, and across the table from Philip his three-hundred-pound brother fed himself with an almost religious devotion.

RALPH MCINERNY, author of the Father Dowling mysteries and other novels, including *Connolly's Life*, *The Noonday Devil*, and *Leave of Absence*, is the Michael P. Grace Professor of Medieval Studies at the University of Notre Dame.

Easeful Death brings back the Knight brothers, Roger and Philip, first encountered in *The Noonday Devil*.